Fun with Jam

The Cameraman – Book 7

Shannon Stiles

Copyright Shannon Stiles 2023

Table of Contents

Chapter 1

Since I'd become a porn producer, I'd *auditioned* a shitload of girls on Sunday afternoons. It was a regular thing, part of my job, which seemed to have evolved into me turning amateur girls who liked to suck and fuck into professional porn stars. And I owed most of my success to the website, *Fukknumzie*, which lets girls post and sell their own videos. Almost all of the girls I produced were making videos to sell on that site.

Nearly all of those girls were pretty nervous when they showed up for their auditions. They knew they were going to have to show their cocksucking skills plus get fucked by a really big dick – mine. That basically was what the auditions were all about – a chance for the girls to prove they could fuck and suck off a big-dick stranger without panicking and freezing up. And a chance for me to spend Sunday afternoons fucking beautiful young women and letting them suck my dick. As far as jobs went, mine was a pretty good one.

Yup, the girls were usually pretty nervous at their auditions, especially at the beginning. Not all of them, of course. There were always exceptions. But few were ever as eager, as ready to go, as Jamie "Stretch" Topin, the beautiful young lady sitting on the couch across from me.

Fuck! She. Was. Gorgeous! Blessed with wide-set green eyes, long, straight, naturally blonde hair, and a face that projected a natural innocence. Add to that what might have been the most alluring mouth I'd ever seen in my life – a perfect cupid's bow upper lip and a plump, pouty lower lip that looked perfect for sucking dicks. Basically, she was a porn producer's dream come true.

And in spite of the *wanna-fuck-me?* smile on her face – tinged with just a touch of nervousness – she looked cute. *Really* cute. And innocent, too. Of course, I knew that wasn't really true. None of the girls who showed up here for a Sunday audition could be described as *innocent.*

"So how old are you, anyway?" I asked her.

"Eighteen, ... plus one month and 17 days. That's old enough, isn't it?" For the first time since she'd showed up, she looked a little anxious.

"Just barely," I told her, offering her a smile at the same time.

She took a deep breath and relaxed. "Good. I thought it was. I would have been here sooner – probably on my birthday – but today was the earliest appointment I could get," she said, adding a giggle.

Did I mention she was cute? Really, really cute? And so, so fuckable. I glanced down at the form where she'd provided personal information, including that her nickname was *Stretch.* "Why do they call you Stretch?"

"Oh, a friend of mine started calling me that when we were grocery shopping one day. She said it was because I couldn't reach items on the top shelves and was always up on my tiptoes, *stretching* to reach them. And it just kinda, ... stuck, you know. Everyone calls me that, now. Even though I'm a little bit taller than I was then."

"Yeah, but c'mon. Stretch Topin? You know what that sounds like, don't you?"

She nodded. "I don't mind. I'm used to it. Actually, I kinda like it – it describes one of my favorite positions."

"Doing yoga?"

The corners of her mouth lifted slightly. "Sure. Yoga."

"And you wanna be a porn star?"

She nodded and nibbled her bottom lip, again showing some nerves.

"You know what porn performers do, don't you?"

"Of course I do. Why would you ask me that?" she said, looking surprised.

"Because you're so young. You've only been legal for ... a month and 17 days. You can't have much experience."

Chapter 2

I picked up a camcorder and aimed it at Jaime as she stood in front of the couch and began to remove her clothes. The great reveal was always one of the highlights of the audition process. What color were her nipples? And pubic hair – did she have any? Or was her snatch completely shaved bald? Or maybe even waxed? There were so many exciting places to check out.

"You're gonna record this?" she said, stopping when she saw what I was doing.

"Yup."

"Why?"

"For my files."

"Are they like, uh, *masturbation* files?"

"What?"

"You know, something for you to watch while you spank your monkey."

"Spank my monkey, huh?" That made me laugh. "Not exactly. But I suppose I could do that if I wanted to. Would you like that? Knowing I was whacking off to video of you stripping naked?"

She paused for just a second. "Yeah, I think I would," she said. "I think knowing I was making you happy would make me happy."

"Good. Because if you decide to go ahead and make videos for Fukknumzie, guys all over the world are gonna be jerking off while watching you have sex."

"It's not a question of *if* I do it. I've already made up my mind. I'm gonna do it. Unless, ..."

"Unless what?"

"Unless I flunk my audition and you don't wanna fuck me." A slightly sad look passed over her face, then quickly disappeared.

"Not much chance of that happening. I already wanna fuck you and I haven't even seen you with your clothes off yet."

"Really? You already wanna fuck me? Even though you haven't seen me naked? I guess that's a good sign but, ... how come?"

"I like your enthusiasm," I told her. "So take off your clothes, do a slow, three-sixty turn, then sit on the couch and spread your legs so I can get a good look at your pussy. *And* record it. Then come back over here and you can fluff up Junior for me."

"Oh boy, oh boy." She peeled off her tank top and dropped her shorts to the floor, revealing that she seemed to have forgotten to wear underwear. No bra. No panties. "I came ready to audition," she said, explaining away her lack of undergarments.

I looked her over, taking my time. Nice tits. A smooth, plump, completely bald pussy. She looked ... delicious. Good enough to eat. And that was definitely on the agenda. "Good. I like girls who are ready to go to work."

"Work? This isn't gonna be work, Charlie. This is gonna be fun."

You bet your sweet, tasty-looking little cunt this is gonna be fun, Jamie. Fucking you is gonna be lotsa fun for me, guaranteed. And hopefully, you'll enjoy it just as much as I will. I sorta get the feeling that'll be the case.

"Okay, just turn around real slowly," I told her.

She did as I instructed but stopped when her back was to me and my camcorder. "You want me to bend over and shake my ass for you?" she said, looking over her shoulder at me. "I've seen that happen in lots of porn videos."

"Sure. Do that."

She widened her stance and bent forward, grasping her legs just below her knees and wiggling her ass at me. Down below, in my shorts, Jumbo, Jr. showed increased interest in the goings-on. I smiled to myself at what a fun Sunday this was turning out to be and moved my camcorder closer to Jamie's wiggling butt.

"Stop wiggling," I told her.

She stopped. "Why?"

Not only was she skillful, she was noisy. Extremely noisy. Loud, *slurpy* noises filled the air as she licked and nibbled and slobbered her way around the head of my dick. She frequently sounded like a small kid trying to suck the last drops of soda out of a glass with a straw.

By the time she moved into power pumping my shaft with her hand while at the same time power pumping my dickhead with her mouth, Jamie's fluffing chore was basically over. Junior was as *fluffy* as he was gonna get – he'd attained maximum fluffiness. Any fluffier and he'd be filling her mouth with dick juice.

"That's good," I told her.

Nothing happened. She didn't stop. Both her hand and her head continued bobbing up and down at a rather rapid rate.

"I'm good. Nice and fluffy," I said.

Nothing. She continued administering what could only be described as a combination handjob-blowjob. And doing a fucking good job of it, too. Too good.

"You keep sucking and I'm gonna cum in your mouth," I warned her.

Finally, she answered me. Her eyes moved up to my face and one of them winked at me as she said, "Mmmmm."

Fuck! This wasn't how I wanted this audition to end. As pretty as Jamie's mouth was, I didn't want to cum in it. At least, not until after I'd tried out her cute little pussy. For size, you know. Kind of a, ... a tightness test, I guess you'd call it. To make sure I'd be able to slam her cunt, repeatedly, without splitting her in two. Or something like that.

Yup, that's what I was thinking – don't use that cum now, save it. Just pull my dick out of that warm, wet suction machine and save it for later. That was the plan. Unfortunately, my dick – Jumbo, Jr. – didn't give a shit about any of that. Not only that, my balls were backing Junior up. As they began to contract, tightening into my body, and Junior began to throb, I realized I was fighting a losing battle. My balls and my dick were conspiring to foil my plan to extract my dick from Jamie's mouth so I could save myself for more fun and games later on.

"Fuck! Final warning. I'm gonna cum," I told her.

Another wink. This one with the other eye. And also, another "Mmmmm."

I grabbed her by the ears and held her head still. "Don't move," I told her. "Hold real still and suck. Just suck."

And as she did that – just sucked – I pumped her mouth full of cum.

Chapter 5

The rest of Jamie's audition took about an hour and a half and pretty much followed the script she'd laid out for me during our little question and answer session. You know. The three things she guessed I might do to her – eat her out, finger-fuck her, and plug her pussy.

So I started by munching her cute little cunt – very tasty, by the way. Sweet. A little hint of ripe banana flavor. I spread it open with my fingers and licked my way up to the top, sucking up the five gallons of pussy juice I encountered along the way. And then I did it again. Many times, in fact.

What? You don't believe me? You think I exaggerated the amount of pussy juice? Okay, I'll admit it – maybe it wasn't *that* much. But she *was* really wet and there *was* a lot. A *lot!*

Each time I arrived at the top of that juicy slit, I paused to take care of that little nubby thing I found waiting for me there. I sucked on it, using just my lips. I tongued it. I pushed her cunt open further – not that easy to do, actually, as wet and slippery as it was – and, treating her clit like the mini-dick it actually was, I gave her a clitoris blowjob. Judging by the way Jamie jerked and bounced around when I did that, plus the moans and swear words that came out of her mouth, she seemed to like it. And for such a young girl, she sure knew a lot of *creative* ways to express her enjoyment.

I followed that up with a little finger-fucking. First with one finger, then with two. When I let my thumb join the fun and romance her clit, she exploded in a shivering, shuddering, shaking, squirming, screaming orgasm that seemed to go on forever.

I waited until she stopped bouncing around and quieted down. And then, just as I was about to launch part three of the script – the part where I took Junior and plugged him into Jamie's 'tiny, tight, almost-*virginal* pussy' – she initiated a change in the schedule.

"I wanna ride," she said. "Can I do that, Charlie? Can I be on top?"

As I believe I've mentioned, I think of myself as a considerate, accommodating person. I like to make my customers happy. *Potential* customers, too. So I said, "Sure," and sat down next to her on the couch.

Without waiting for further confirmation, she pushed me down so that I was lying across the couch, on my back. She crawled up on top of me, stopping briefly on her way up to offer Junior two quick licks and a long, milking suck. Then she patted him on the head and said, "That's nice."

Junior nodded his agreement. Vigorously. And I agreed with both of them – that *was* nice.

"This is my all-time favorite position," she told me, continuing her crawl until her cunt was poised directly over her target.

"How come?"

"Because guys last longer when they're on the bottom." She reached down and wiped my dickhead back and forth along her juicy slit a couple of times, then slipped it in and slowly sank all the way down into my pubes. "Oh fucking boy!" she said in a soft voice as she sat on top of me, not moving. "That's a cuntful!"

I smiled at her colorful language. You'd think a young girl like Jamie, with limited experience, wouldn't be able to so easily handle a dick as big as mine. But there she was, sitting on top of me, Junior plugged as far up her cunt as it was possible for him to go, and she was smiling back at me.

"You comfortable?" I asked her.

"Uh-huh. It feels, ... good."

"I'm surprised."

"Why?"

"Most girls have trouble with Junior's size. At least, in the beginning."

"I told you, Charlie, I've been practicing."

"With your dildo. Right?"

"Yup. Ten inches of fun. And really thick, too. It's the thickness that takes getting used to, you know. Not the length." She leaned forward and began to slowly rock back and forth, letting Junior slide in and out of her wet, slippery pussy.

"Fuck, you're tight!" I grasped her by the hips, lifting her up into the air a few inches, then letting her slide back down. Then I did it again. And again. Junior seemed to like that. I know I did – Jamie's slick, silky pussy felt like a little piece of heaven.

"Mmm," she said, gradually picking up speed. "Junior would make any pussy feel tight."

"He *is* kinda large," I agreed.

"Large?" The rocking of her pelvis morphed into more of a *rock 'n roll* motion as she squirmed around on my dick. "Fuck! Junior's not large. He's a *monster!* A great, big, wonderful, ... *monster!*"

I laughed as I assisted by holding her in place, helping her fuck me. "You're gonna embarrass him, saying stuff like that."

"It's the truth. And I've wanted to do this – to do *you* – for so long. *Soooo* long."

"And now you are."

"Mmm, yeah. Now I am." She leaned forward even more, pressing her breasts into my chest, just letting her hips and ass take over essential duties as she twerked on my dick.

For the next few minutes, I really didn't have to do much of anything. She did all the work necessary to induce an orgasm in each of us, slipping and sliding and bouncing around on my dick. She was so active up there on top, I began to worry she might actually vault off me and end up on the floor. To ensure that didn't happen, I wrapped my arms around her and held her in place. Then I just lay there, concentrating on making sure Junior stayed hard as Jamie's cunt assaulted him. That wasn't much of a problem, actually. Making sure Junior kept his *head* in the game, I mean.

When she came this time, it was different. Quieter. Gentler. There were none of the gymnastic gyrations she'd exhibited when she'd rode my fingers to orgasm a few minutes earlier. Apparently, she'd used up all her energy bouncing around on my dick because she just held me tight, moaned, and *vibrated* for about 30 seconds while juice leaked out of her cunt, spreading the smell of bananas throughout my living room.

Evidently, the combination of vibrations and the scent of ripe bananas was all it took to push Junior over the edge. Fifteen seconds into Jamie's orgasm, with absolutely zero warning from my balls, my friendly little cum cannon began firing spurt after spurt of hot, sticky fuck-juice into her tight, silky pussy. I grabbed her by the ass, pulled her tightly against me, and held her there until she stopped shaking and Junior ran out of ammunition.

"Mmm, good," she mumbled, collapsing on top of me.

Yup. It *was* good. Jamie was good. Her performance was good. Really, really, *really* good! So good, in fact, that it belonged in a special category, one populated by only a few, *special* girls. I called that category, ... *Best Auditions Ever!*

Chapter 6

"So, ... lemme just make sure I understand this *special* you're offering me."

"Sure, ask me anything. But it's not just for you, Jamie. It's our standard contract for newcomers."

We were sitting on my couch, relaxing with beers and weed after a long afternoon of sucking and fucking, followed by a shower together that had degenerated into some serious hanky-panky. I didn't know how Jamie felt, but I was pooped. The Sunday afternoon display of her talents had pretty much exhausted me – in a good way. I was looking forward to a good night's sleep. But first, we had business to take care of.

"Okay, then. It's a thousand to get started. Right?"

"That's right. But you don't have to pay up front. You can pay a hundred a month for 10 months. No interest."

"And for this I get 15 videos to sell on Fukknumzie?"

"Yup. Plus a sample video you can give away for free to interest potential customers. Typically, we make five different videos, each one concentrating on a different position – a blowjob video, missionary, doggy style, cowgirl, and reverse cowgirl. If you want, we can combine cowgirl and reverse cowgirl into one video and you can do anything you want for the final one.

"Anyway, after we finish recording each position, I'll edit the footage into three different videos – one seven minutes long, one at 12 minutes, and one about 20. So you'll get three videos of each of the five positions as well as the sample video. Total of 16."

"And I get to set my own prices for the videos?"

"Yup."

"And you're gonna take 15 percent of my sales for the first two years and after that I get to keep it all, right?

"Yup. But that's just for the sale of the videos *I* produce. You can sell anything else you want – used panties, personally autographed photos, videos that someone else makes for you, whatever – and I don't take any of that. You keep 100 percent."

She grinned. "Used panties?"

"Hey, don't knock it. They're a big-ticket item on Fukknumzie. And the longer a girl claims to have worn them, the more they sell for. A popular girl can sell panties she's worn for three consecutive days for hundreds of dollars. Guys think those smell *better* than one or two-day panties."

Jamie shook her head and laughed. "Guys are gross, Charlie. You know that?"

Oh, yeah. I know that, sweetie. Guys <u>are</u> gross. I'm pretty sure most girls would be really surprised at some of the thoughts that flit through the average guy's head.

That's what I was thinking. And even though I knew her question was rhetorical in nature, I answered it, anyway. "Gross? Yeah, I guess we are. Maybe."

"No maybe about it. You are."

"But in a good way. Right?"

She slapped my shoulder and displayed her huge grin. "So that's it," she said. "That's pretty much all I need to know. It all sounds good. Let's do it."

"Great. So now, let me ask *you* a few questions. Okay?"

"Sure. Ask me anything."

"Well, first off, I guess – whaddaya do, Jamie?"

"Do? Pretty much whatever I want to," she said, giggling. "My stepmom's really lenient."

"You live with your stepmother?"

"Yeah, mostly. I never knew my real mom. She took off right after I was born. Hasn't been heard from since." She paused her narrative long enough to take a massive hit from the joint we were sharing, then handed it to me and continued.

"But now my dad and stepmom are divorced and I live with my stepmom because, well, I've known her practically all my life and it's kinda like *she's* my real mom. You know?"

"Uh-huh. I think I do," I said.

"Sometimes I stay with my dad, though. Usually when my stepmom and I are fighting about something. But they're both pretty nice people, actually."

"I see." I took a hit off the joint. "Anyway, I meant for work. What do you do for work?"

"Oh. I'm a student."

"Trade school? College?"

"High school."

I almost choked. A noticeable *gulping* sound escaped from from my throat. Had I just gotten sucked off by and then gone on to fuck a high school student? "But you *are* really 18, though. Right?"

"Yeah. I am. Plus one month and 17 days." She took a sip of her beer.

Great. She was legal. Realizing I'd been holding my breath while awaiting Jamie's answer, I exhaled.

"But I'm going to summer school because a couple of the classes I needed to graduate didn't count and I had to take them over."

"Yeah? How come they didn't count?"

"Oh, I got in a little trouble with a couple of the teachers. Mr. Thompson and Mr. Glenn. History and English. I have to repeat those two classes even though I got an A in both of them the first time. It's really not fair – all we were doing was texting."

"Uh-huh," I said, taking a hit off the joint. I was beginning to get the gist of Jamie's story.

"And emailing."

"Uh-huh."

"There might have been something about some photo exchanges, too. Something like that – I can't remember exactly what evidence they had, they had *soooo* much."

"The school, you mean?" I took another hit and passed the joint over to her.

She took a big hit, held it for a few seconds, then blew it out toward the ceiling. "Yeah, the school. And the police, too. They were a real pain in the ass, the cops. So many questions."

"Wow. So this was really like, a big deal, then."

"Yeah, it was. And the upshot of the whole deal was that I had to repeat those two classes in order to graduate."

"What happened to the two teachers?"

She shrugged. "Mr. Thompson and Mr. Glenn? I don't know. They're not around anymore. Too bad, too. I kinda miss them. They gave me extra attention and like, special tutoring and stuff. And they promised me I'd get an A in their classes. And I did, too, for a while. But then I didn't, you know?"

"Uh-huh."

"I really miss Mr. Glenn. He was super ... nice."

"What did your parents have to say about all this, anyway?" I asked her.

"Not much. My stepmom said not to send naked pictures of myself to my teachers and my dad told me not to accept naked pictures from them, either. Teachers, I mean. No naked pics, either way. And then Daddy said that when I finally got my diploma at the end of summer school, he'd buy me a new car. So, yay to that. Cool, huh?"

"Yeah, cool." Fuck! This girl, Jamie, was so young. I felt guilty, like I was taking advantage of her – of her youth, of her naivete, of her love for my dick. But of course, when you get right down to it, that's what I do with all the girls who come through here. I take advantage of them. It's the reason I started this business, after all. So I could score a lot of pussy. And if I do say so, myself, in addition to being a successful business, it has done exactly that – provided me with an endless stream of tight, juicy cunts attached to beautiful young women who were eager to make a lot of money by showing off their *goodies* and demonstrating their *talents* on Fukknumzie dot com. *And* pay me for the privilege of letting me fuck them silly and video it. All because I was born with a giant dick.

Fuck! Was this the best of all possible worlds or what!

Chapter 7

It was after dark when Jamie left. I ordered an Uber for her, then walked her down to the parking lot. We stood there, talking, waiting for the car to show up.

"So, I'll see you on Tuesday, then," she said. "About seven."

"Yup."

"Still here, at your apartment. Right?"

"Yup. We'll do the sample video right here. In my living room, just like today. But then we'll have to skip a week while we're moving into our new studio and getting things set up. After that, it'll be every Tuesday evening until we finish."

"So I'm gonna have to miss a week, huh?"

"Yup. We're fixing the place up next week. Me and Joey. You know who that is, right?"

"He's that blonde, surfer dude who's in some of the videos with you, right?"

"Yeah. But he's not really a surfer. He just looks like one."

"Am I gonna meet him?"

"You certainly are. And if you want to, you can suck his dick and fuck him, too."

"Really?"

"Yup."

"Oh boy, oh boy! Two big dicks for the price of one!"

"You like your big dicks, don't you, Jamie?"

She bounced up and down on her toes a couple of times and she smiled. "I do. I like 'em big. *Big!*"

"I thought so," I said, smiling back at her.

"You know the guy I mentioned? Mr. Glenn?"

"Your teacher?"

"My English teacher, yeah. He had a big dick. *Really* big."

"You don't say."

33

"I do say. It was almost as big as yours, Charlie. You know, you should hire him to work at your new studio. I bet he'd make a great porn actor. And he probably needs a new job, too. I don't think they're gonna let him be a teacher anymore."

"Sure, maybe. I probably will need at least one more guy once we get the new place up and running. If you see him, tell him to call me and set up an audition."

"Ooh, an audition. Does that mean he's gonna have to suck you off and fuck you?" she said, laughing.

I laughed along with her. "Hardly. I'll get a girl to audition him. Maybe Joey's girlfriend, Megan."

"I could do it, you know. Audition him for you, I mean. Oh boy, I'd be glad to. I never actually got to, ... *do* anything with him, you know. Just look at pictures."

"Well, we'll see what happens if any of this comes about."

"Yeah. I don't know where he is, anyway." She looked pensive for a moment, then said, "So tell me about your new studio, Charlie. That's where I'll be making most of my videos, right?"

"Yup. I bought a house and me and Joey have been renovating it. Turning it into a porn studio."

"You bought a *house*?"

"Yup." I nodded, feeling proud of myself. I was growing up. I owned a house. Well, me and the bank, anyway.

"Here? In town?"

"No. In Shegley. I couldn't afford a place here." Shegley was a small, unincorporated community a few miles down the road, heading inland. In addition to lower real estate prices, it offered the advantage of being unzoned, meaning I could use the house to operate a business. Which was exactly what I was planning to do.

"Shit! I'm surprised you could afford a place *anywhere* around here. How'd you swing that?"

"Well, I had some money saved up. And I got a small business loan for the down payment. Actually, my company owns the house."

"A small business loan? Like, from a local bank?"

"Technically, from the government."

"Really? They gave you a loan for a porn business?"

"I'm not a porn business, Jamie. I'm a Digital Video Production, Editing, and Distribution business. That's what I put in the block that said, *Type of Business.*"

"I guess, then, that makes me a *video actress*, yeah?"

"Exactly."

"So what's the name of your business, Charlie?"

"Jumbo Johnson Productions."

"You should call it *Jumbo's Fuck Factory*. That's a better name."

I chuckled. "I'd probably have to pay the loan back right away if I did that."

She leaned close to me and grasped the front of my shorts, in the process encasing a limp, sleeping Junior in her fingers. "Did I ever tell you I love your dick, Charlie?"

"I think you did."

"I'm gonna miss him, you know." She squeezed her fingers, causing Junior to shake himself awake.

"You'll be back here on Tuesday," I told her. "That's only two days from now."

"Yeah, but then I'll have to go two weeks with no Junior. I'm gonna be *soooo* lonesome." She squeezed, again. Junior stretched and began to stand up.

"Well, if you want to, you can drop by every night and suck me to sleep. How does that sound?"

"Really? Oh boy, oh boy! That sounds, ... *wonderful!*" Her squeezes started to feel suspiciously like a fabric-wrapped handjob.

"I'm kidding, Jamie. We can't do that."

"Why not?"

"I'm busy at night. Working."

"Fucking other pussies, you mean."

"Yeah, that's what I do. That's my job – you know that."

"I guess so." She looked sad. But then, suddenly, her face brightened. "Hey, I've got an idea," she said.

"Yeah? What?"

"Junior's getting hard, you know."

"I know. That's your fault. You're playing with him."

"So how about I give you a quickie blowjob? Just suck you off real quick? Wouldn't you like that?"

"Well, yeah. I would. But we're in the middle of a parking lot, Jamie."

She looked around, as if she just realized where we were, and then she giggled. "Oh, yeah. We are, aren't we. But it's dark. And we could move over there, next to those cars, and no one would be able to see us. I promise I'll make it quick, Charlie."

It wasn't often I was put in the position of having to dissuade a gorgeous young babe from sucking my dick. Like I've said, I'm an accommodating type of guy. And the idea of a sneaky blowjob in the middle of a parking lot, where we might get caught, sounded kinda, ... *exciting*.

Fortunately, I was saved from making a potentially bad decision by the arrival of the Uber. I pulled away from Jamie's grasp and adjusted my package, making it less noticeable. "Looks like your ride's here," I told her, nodding at the approaching car.

"Bummer," she said.

"Yeah, bummer." It was, too. For both of us, apparently.

As the Uber came to a stop next to us, she reached up, wrapped her arms around my neck, and kissed me. "See you Tuesday, then."

"Yup. Tuesday." I opened the car door and helped her inside, giving her ass a friendly squeeze as I did so and getting a grin in return. She made herself comfortable, gave me a little wave, and I slammed the door shut, returning her wave. Then I stood back and watched as the car drove away, taking with it what had to be one of the horniest girls in the entire world.

Oh boy, oh boy, as Jamie might say. I could hardly wait for Tuesday and a chance to tap that fine, eager-to-fuck piece of ass again. That was gonna *soooo* much fun.

Oh boy!

Chapter 8

Jamie showed up right on time Tuesday evening, anxious to get to work. We sat on the couch, relaxing with a beer and a smoke while I explained what we were going to do – make a *casting* video. Just a little sample of some of the things Jamie was willing to do in order to attain porn stardom on Fukknumzie dot com.

"So, basically," I was telling her, "after you come in, have a seat on the couch, then face the big camera. I'll sit in my recliner over there and ask you some questions."

She scooted over, closer to me, and dropped her hand into my lap, slowly rubbing her hand over the front of my shorts in what felt like a search for Junior.

I removed her hand and placed it back in her own lap, saying, "Save that for later."

"Save what?" she said, giving me an innocent look.

"You know *what*, Jamie. Your hand on the front of my shorts."

"I was just smoothing them out for you."

"Uh-huh."

"I *was*. They were wrinkled. Badly wrinkled." She smiled at me, leaned back and pulled her hair back behind her shoulders, then fluffed it out with both hands. "So anyway, what kind of questions are you gonna ask me?"

"Just some things about your sexual experience, why you want to be a porn actress, stuff like that."

She nodded, appearing serious. "Should I lie or tell the truth?"

"It's always better to tell the truth, Jamie. It's easier to remember the truth than a lie."

She turned her head and grinned at me. "So when you ask me why I want to be a porn star, I –"

"Don't say *porn star*. Don't call yourself that – some guys don't like it. Say you're a porn actress, not a porn star."

39

"Oh, okay. "So when you ask me why I want to be a porn *actress*, I should tell the truth?"

"Absolutely. The truth is always better. It will even set you free, they say."

"Yeah, so will turning 18," she mumbled. "Anyway, so then, I should just answer that the reason I want to be a porn actress is so I can suck that giant dick of yours, right? And fuck it, too, because I've been in love with your dick for like, forev –"

"About a month and a half," I said. "And you know, it might be all right to lie just a little bit." I demonstrated how much that was, using my thumb and my forefinger. "Maybe just say that you like big dicks in general, instead of saying you like *my* big dick."

"Oh, sure. I can do that. That's not even a lie."

"Good."

"Is that it? Is that all you're gonna ask me?"

"Pretty much. And a little about what kind of sexual activities you enjoy. And what you're willing to do on camera. That's pretty much it."

"I like just about every kind of sexual activity," she said. "And you can film any of it. I don't care."

"Great. So just tell me that when I ask you."

"Okay. And then what?"

"I'll tell you what to do as we go along. First, I'll talk you out of your clothes and then I'll convince you to to give me a blowjob, to fluff up Junior. Pretty much the same as we did on Sunday."

"Oh boy! But you don't have to *convince* me, Charlie."

"Yeah, I do. Because in the video we'll be making, I want you to pretend to be this shy, innocent young girl who's not sure she wants to do any of these nasty things and I have to talk her into doing stuff. So I don't have to convince *you*, I have to convince *her*."

"Oh, okay. I get it." She hit the joint, held it for a few seconds, then exhaled toward that dark spot on my ceiling, just like everyone does. Even me.

"It's gonna be just like your audition," I told her. "Only we'll be videoing everything."

"Is your friend, Joey, gonna show up tonight? To help with the camera work?"

"No, it's just you and me, tonight. This whole video takes place right here, on this couch, with just the two of us. We don't need Joey for this. I'm gonna shoot most of it with my big camera, here, at a medium distance. Only a little bit of closeup work, using my camcorder. That way, if guys wanna see your pussy up close or watch closeups of my dick sliding in and out of it, they'll have to cough up some loose change for one of your other videos. One of your 15 specialty videos."

"That sounds good, I guess."

"Yup. It is. So basically, it'll just be me asking you what things you're willing to do. You know – will you take on two guys at the same time, are you willing to take a dick up your ass, stuff like that. Then you act like you're thinking about it but it kinda scares you a little bit, okay? And eventually you either agree to do it or you don't. It's up to you – just tell me the truth."

"I'm gonna agree to everything, you know," she said.

"I know you are, sweetie. And that's why I also know you're gonna be a huge success on Fukknumzie and make a shitload of money."

"I hope you're right, Charlie."

"I am. Okay, so, ... lemme just go over this with you one more time. You ring the bell and I'll answer the door. You ask me if I'm Mr. Johnson and I'll say, 'I am. But call me Jumbo.' Something like that. Then you introduce yourself and, ... who *are* you, anyway? What's your name?"

"What?" she said, looking confused. "Me? I'm, uh, ... *Jamie.*"

"No, I mean, what name are you gonna use for your videos? You don't wanna use your real name – it makes it too easy for stalkers to find you."

"Stalkers? What?"

"Yeah. There are wackos out there who will see your videos and convince themselves the two of you are in love. They'll download all your videos, order your photos and used panties and anything else you sell, and eventually they'll try to strike up a personal relationship with you. So to protect your identity – to make sure they don't show up at your house with flowers – you need a fake identity to use on Fukknumzie. A *porn* name."

"Oh. I, ... I didn't think of that. I don't have one."

"So let's make one up. Any ideas?"

"I think maybe I'd like to be a, ..."

"What?" I said, when she didn't finish the sentence.

"Stella."

"Stella?"

"Yeah. I've always liked that name."

"Okay, *Stella*, finish your beer and let's get going. Let's make some *porn!*"

"I'm ready." She drained her beer and stood up. As she headed down the short hallway toward my front door, I heard her say, "Oh boy, oh boy, oh boy!"

Yup. Jamie was ready. Definitely ready.

Chapter 9

Two Tuesdays later, Jamie showed up at our new studio in Shegley, ready to begin shooting her *specialty* videos. The ones that were going to make her a lot of money. There was no doubt in my mind about that – Jamie was going to make a *lot* of money selling video downloads.

I'd helped her set up her account on Fukknumzie dot com and her first video, the free-to-watch-or-download *casting* video I'd made for her, was already up there and getting a lot of interest. She wasn't making any money yet, of course, but the end of the video had a nice graphic that read, *More fun with Stella coming <u>real</u> soon. Check back often.* I was positive that, a couple of months for now, a talented girl like Jamie would be raking in the old dough-re-mi. The moolah. The bread. Bundles of cash.

"This is nice," she said, glancing around the living room. "Except for all these lights and cameras and stuff, it looks just like a regular house."

"Yup. That's the look I was going for."

"Three bedrooms?"

"Yup. The master bedroom is the studio. One of the others is a sound recording and editing room and the other one is a recovery room."

"A recovery room?" She looked puzzled. "You're not doing surgery here, too, are you?"

I chuckled. "No, it's for anyone who wants to rest, take a nap, whatever. There's a couple of single beds in there."

"That's nice, I guess. So where are you gonna sleep, then?"

"Oh, I'm not gonna live here. I'm keeping my apartment. This place is strictly for making videos."

"It looks great, Charlie. It really does."

"Wait'll you see the master bath – it's huge. And there's a fucking gigantic walk-in shower, too. Big enough for four or five people to take a shower together. You girls are gonna love cleaning up in it, there's so much room. And I can see myself shooting some future scenes in there, also."

Calm down, came a warning from the little voice in my head. *I mean, I know you're excited about your new place, but jeez, ...*

"You should definitely do that," she said. "Fucking in the shower is lots of fun," she said.

"Yeah? And just how do you know that, young lady?"

She smiled her best *innocent* smile. "So I've heard."

I steered her over to a seat on the couch, grabbed a couple of beers from the kitchen, and joined her.

"Thanks," she said when I handed a beer to her. "You're not gonna show me the studio?"

"You'll see it in a few minutes. Except for the lights and cameras, it looks just like a bedroom. There's a king-sized bed and some furniture and stuff."

"Okay, then." She took a sip of her beer. "You still keep your stash box under the couch?"

"Yup. I do."

She leaned over and groped around under the couch for a bit, finally sitting back up with the box. Opening it, she pulled out a joint and a couple of lighters. She placed one lighter on my thigh, put my stash box on the coffee table in front of us, and fired up the joint, taking a big hit before passing it to me. "This is just like in your apartment," she said, exhaling. "Are you gonna do auditions here, now? On this couch?"

I took a hit. "Haven't completely decided about that yet. Probably not. I'm leaning toward still doing them at my apartment."

"Yeah. That makes more sense, actually. That way you won't have to drive seven or eight miles, all the way over here to Shegley, to get your dick sucked on Sunday afternoons. You can do it at home."

I glanced over at her. She was grinning at me. "Exactly what I've been thinking," I told her.

The sound of a door opening and then closing drifted into the living room from down the hall, making Jamie look in that direction. "Was that your door?" she said.

"Yup."

"You don't lock it?"

"I do. Sometimes. But that's Joey. He has a key."

At almost the exact time, Joey walked into the living room. He stopped when he saw the two of us sitting on the couch and said, "Hey, guys. Started without me, I see."

I nodded. "Yup. You're late. Come on over here and meet Jamie."

Jamie leaned forward as he approached and they shook hands. "Nice to finally meet you," she said.

"You, too. Lemme just go get a beer and then I'll come back and we can get better acquainted, okay?"

"Sure."

"Be right back," he said, heading for the kitchen.

"So what are we gonna do tonight, Charlie?" Jamie said.

"Usually, we start with missionary. There'll be some foreplay at the beginning – some kissing and some groping, maybe. You suck my dick, I eat your pussy. Like that. And then I'll fuck you in a couple of different positions and we'll wrap it up with a nice scene of me cumming in your mouth. That's the plan. But it's your video. We can do whatever you want."

"You're gonna fuck me in a couple of different positions? I thought missionary *was* the position."

"Yeah, well, that just means we're face to face when we're fucking. But we can vary it a bit. Make it a little more interesting."

"Okay, that sounds good. What about Joey?"

"What about him?"

"Is he here as a performer or as your camera guy?"

"That's up to you, too. Do you want him in your videos?"

"Sure. Two dicks are better than one, don'cha think?"

Our conversation was interrupted by Joey's return. He took a seat on the other side of Jamie and said, "So, what are we talking about?"

"You," I told him.

"Yeah? What about me?"

"Jamie wants you to be in her videos. You up for that?"

He reached down and squeezed his dick through his shorts. "Up? Not yet," he said, a huge grin on his face. "But Jamie can probably fix that for me. Right, Jamie?"

"Pretty sure I can." She reached over and added a squeeze of her own to the front of his shorts. "But I need to check this out first, you know. So, ... how about you take your shorts off and let me see your equipment?"

"My equipment, huh?" he said, chuckling as he unzipped his shorts and slid them down, revealing his semi-erect dick. "There you go. Whaddaya think?"

"Hmm," she said, studying his dick. "Not very firm."

"That's where you come in. Making him firm is *your* job."

She reached over and wrapped her fingers around the shaft of his not-very-firm dick, then leaned down and nuzzled his dickhead with her lips. "Like this, you mean?"

Joey jerked and his dick stiffened. "Yeah. That's a good start."

"Jamie, don't," I told her.

It looked as if she was just about to slurp Joey's dick into her mouth but she stopped and looked back at me. "Don't what?" she said.

"Don't do that now. Save it for the video."

"Okay. But I just wanna see what it tastes like, you know." She leaned back down, doing exactly what I asked her not to do – slurping his dick into her mouth and gifting it with a couple of quick head bobs. When she released him and sat back up, Joey's dick was completely firm and she was smiling. "Tastes great," she said.

Down in my own pants, Junior, sensing what was going on around him, began to wake up. He pushed against the inside of my shorts, obviously eager to get outside and join the fun. Before things could get out of hand, though, I said, "C'mon, Joey. Take a couple of hits, finish your beer, and let's get to work."

"Yeah," Jamie said. "Let's get going. Oh boy! Two dicks for little old me to play with. Oh boy, oh boy, oh boy, I can hardly wait!"

Chapter 10

Jamie didn't have long to wait. We began her first for-sale video with her lying on her back on the brand new bed in my brand new studio, completely naked, playing with her pussy. My main camera – also brand new – was set on a tripod at the side of the bed, recording her. At the same time, Joey walked around the bed with a camcorder, shooting the scene from various angles.

"Okay, I'm gonna go out in the hall and close the door now," I told him. Then I'm gonna open it and come back into the room. So aim your camcorder at the door and catch me as I come in. Okay?"

"No problem." He gave me a thumbs up.

I went out, closed the door briefly, then opened it again and walked into the room. Joey tracked my movements as I crossed over to the bed and stopped, looking down at Jamie as she diddled her cunt with her fingers. "Hi," I said to her.

"Hi, Charlie." She smiled up at me.

"Wait, wait," I said. "Remember, I'm not Charlie – I'm Jumbo Johnson. My dick is Jumbo Johnson, Jr. if you wanna call him by his full name, or just Junior for short. And you're Stella. Okay?"

She giggled. "Whoops! I forgot. Sorry. Can we fix it?"

"Sure. No biggie. We'll just do it again and I'll edit that part out."

"Okay."

"And here we go." I said hi to her again.

She smiled at me again and continued stroking her pussy. "Hi, Jumbo. What's up?"

"Nothing's *up*, right now. But I was hoping you could fix that."

"Yeah? I guess I might be able to help you out. What did you have in mind?"

"This," I said. I pulled my T-shirt off over my head, dropped my shorts and boxers to the floor, and clambered up onto the bed.

Kneeling next to Jamie's head, I dangled my mostly limp dick over her mouth.

"Oh, that," she said, ogling Junior and licking her lips. "Sure. I can definitely help you out with *that*."

"Good." I swung one leg over her so that I was straddling her, almost sitting on her upper chest and tits.

She reached behind her and pulled the pillow out from under her head, folded it in half, then tucked it back into place. "That's better," she said, wrapping her hand around my dick and lightly massaging it. "Hi there, Junior."

I adjusted my position slightly, making it even easier for Jamie to reach her intended target. "Junior says hi," I said.

"What's the matter, Junior?" she said, stroking him and talking to him. It looked as if she was talking into a microphone. "Have you got a case of the limpies?"

Joey chuckled at her choice of terminology and moved in for a closeup as she tugged my dickhead partway into her mouth, teasing the tip with her tongue. Junior jumped, his *limpies* evidently forgotten, and he temporarily escaped from between her lips. I pushed him back in and told her, "Suck it, Stella. Suck it good!"

"Mmmmm," she said, doing as I asked. She sucked. She slurped. She slurnched. That's a word I invented. It means to slurp and munch on a dickhead at the same time. Not that easy to do, I've been told, but Jamie, in her role as Stella, was doing a terrific job of it.

"Give me your camcorder," I said to Joey.

He handed it to me and I aimed it down at Jamie, getting a nice POV closeup of Junior sliding in and out of her mouth while drool ran down the sides of her cheeks. "Go stand in the hall and slide the doors closed and when I yell, come in and walk over here, say hi to us, then take off your clothes and join us."

"Whaddaya gonna yell?" Joey said.

Although Joey was a helluva nice guy, he wasn't the brightest bulb in the room. "Oh, I don't know. Maybe something like, ... *COME IN!!*" I said.

"That'll work." He ducked through the bedroom door and closed it behind him.

"Keep sucking, Stella. Keep sucking until Joey comes back and joins us."

"En feb wup?" she mumbled around my dick.

"What?"

"Wub bappinz abfa vap? Abfa Fowee pumz bab."

I had no clue what she was trying to say to me – realistically, talking with a mouthful of dick wasn't a very good way to make oneself understood. Even so, I had a pretty good idea of what might be on her mind, so I told her, "After Joey joins us, you just keep both of our dicks happy for a few minutes, get 'em nice and firm, all fluffed up and ready to go, and then we'll move right into missionary. All right?"

She nodded, the back and forth motion of her head producing a very ... *soothing* feeling in my balls.

"Do you want just one of us to fuck you or both of us?" I asked her.

"Mofe!" The answer came roaring out of her mouth, only slightly distorted by my dick. But she said it so forcefully that in the process, she accidentally bit my dickhead. Hard.

I jerked back and tried to pull my dick out of her mouth but Jamie held on tight, refusing to release me. Truthfully, I was upset. Junior, having taken the blow right in the head, so to speak, was pissed, as well. I said, "Ouch!" for both of us.

"I'b vollee," she said. I was pretty sure that was supposed to be an apology but I didn't believe she was really sorry, that she really meant it. That was probably because she was giggling into my dick as she said it. Those giggles felt pretty good, actually. A lot better than the bite.

As payback, I reached behind me and pinched her nipple. Hard, too, twisting it back and forth between my thumb and my index finger.

The results, however, were not what I expected. Instead of reacting with an expression of pain, Jamie moaned in ecstasy.

I knew I'd have to edit out the last few minutes – I doubted many viewers of porn would be interested in watching girls bite guys' dicks. Of course, I could be wrong. Maybe they would. Maybe dick biting would become the *next big thing* in porn because it gets super popular with women and ends up being the world's favorite kind of porn. If so, someday some enterprising porn producer was probably going to make a gazillion bucks as the genius who discovered what kind of porn women *really* like. But it wasn't going to be me. And it wasn't going to start with this video.

And I could see that shit getting out of hand, too. Dick biting, I mean. Over time, bites getting harder and harder. Eventually drawing blood. And then, finally, there'd be a whole new category of videos – vampire cocksucker porn!

Yup, I was definitely gonna have to cut the bite scene. Not a biggie, really. I always had to edit out the chatter and directions I gave the girls – and Joey, too – that went on when we were shooting. I try to edit out the use of Joey's name, too, but I guess I must have missed it a few times because most regular Fukknumzie patrons seem to know what it is. I've told him a dozen times that he needs a fake name, a *porn* name, but he insists that as long as he keeps his last name private, using his real first name is fine.

I looked down at Jamie, shooting video of her as she held Junior in her hand and slurnched his head. She'd certainly done a good job of fluffing him up – he was essentially the doppelganger of a steel rod. I pushed her hand aside and slid that bad boy deep into her throat, then pulled him out and did it again, over and over. Once I had several seconds of that recorded, I aimed my camcorder at the door. "JOEY!" I called. "COME IN!"

Chapter 11

Joey opened the door and came into the room, crossing over to the bed where I was still face-fucking Jamie. He and I had performed some version of this scene with dozens of girls during the past couple of years, so it wasn't as if he needed direction from me. We both knew what to do.

"Hey, Stella," he said, standing next to the bed and watching as she repeatedly tried – and failed – to swallow my dick. "Wha'cha doing?"

"Vlaying," she mumbled.

"Yeah? Looks like fun. Can I vlay with you guys?"

"Thuah!" she said.

I flinched at the force with which she agreed to let Joey 'vlay' with us but thankfully, no dick bites were forthcoming.

Joey stripped off his clothes, tossed them onto a nearby chair, and climbed up onto the bed with us. Jamie immediately abandoned her efforts to gobble my entire dick, rolled over toward Joey, and pulled *his* dick into her mouth. And since I was the one holding the camcorder, I was forced to shoot the video of Junior's humiliating rejection.

Except, as it turned out, it wasn't a rejection at all. After just a few seconds of munching Joey's dick – all it took to make it nice and firm and ready to *perform* – she released it, grasped Junior again, and tugged him closer to her. Since Junior and I always travel together, I ended up closer to her, as well.

With my dick in one hand and Joey's in her other hand, she dragged each of them to the front of her mouth, where her tongue could reach them both at the same time. And then she tasted our dickheads. And kissed them. And nibbled them. She stuck out her tongue and ran it back and forth from one dickhead to the other in long, slurpy licks, causing me to shudder and making Joey moan with pleasure. I still found it hard to believe that a girl with Jamie's limited experience could be such a skillful cocksucker.

53

There really wasn't any point in letting Jamie continue to play with our dicks, though. Both of those fuck-sticks were as firm as they were going to get. But her tongue on my dickhead felt *soooo* good, ... and I knew this would look good in the video, too, so I let it go on for longer than I should have. Several minutes, actually. Until Joey expressed concern.

"Uh, this isn't supposed to be a cumshot scene, is it?" he asked me.

"What? No, she's just fluffing us up."

"I'm pretty fluffy already. Much fluffier and I'm gonna spill my load right into Jamie's mouth."

Jamie paused what appeared to be a failing effort to stuff both of our dickheads into her mouth at the same time and looked up at us. "I'm good with that," she said.

"Don't do it, Joey," I told him. "Save it. If you've really gotta cum, wait until I'm fucking her and then let her suck you off. I'll pull her down to the end of the bed so that her legs are hanging over it and I can fuck her standing up. That way I'll be able to get POV shots of her cunt swallowing my dick over and over. Then I'll just pan up her body and we'll find you kneeling over her face, your dick in her mouth. Just let me get a few seconds of you face-fucking her, then go ahead and cum in her mouth."

"Oh boy! That sounds good," Jamie said.

"Yeah, sounds good to me, too," Joey added, nodding his head. "But let's make it quick, okay? I'm really ready to pop and I'm not gonna last much longer."

"You know you're gonna have to cum again later, at the end of the evening. Right?"

"Yeah, yeah. I know. The big double cumshot scene to end the video. Don't worry. I'll be ready."

"Is that tonight?" Jamie said. "A double cumshot scene?"

"Yup. It is."

"To my face?"

"Yup."

"Oh boy!"

"Actually, we're probably gonna end every session with you taking a double cumshot to your face. That's what we usually do when we're using both of us."

"Really?"

"Really. Guys who pay to download your videos won't be satisfied unless they see cum all over your face and your mouth full of it."

A big grin came over her face. "Oh boy, oh boy, oh boy!" she said. "This is gonna be *soooo* much fun!"

"You like cum, do you, Jamie?" Joey asked her.

"I do, I do. I love it. I *love* cum. The more the merrier. If I had six guys cumming on me, cumming *in* me, I'd be six times as happy as just having one guy."

"Fuck, Jamie, I like sex, but you're just nuts!" he said.

She nodded in agreement. "Yeah, I am. I admit it. I'm crazy for cum. I really, *really* love it.!"

"Okay, then," I said. "Let's get into this next scene so Joey can get his dick drained and you can get some of that cum you love so much. Scoot down to the end of the bed and drape your legs over the end so I can fuck you while I'm standing up."

She did as instructed but when I attempted to line Junior up with her cunt, I discovered she was too low. "Pussy's not high enough," I told Joey. "Toss me a couple pillows."

Two pillows came flying toward me from the other end of the bed. I snatched them out of the air. "Lift your ass up, sweetie, so I can get you in position to plug that tight little cunt of yours," I said.

She giggled and pulled her legs up and rocked backward, lifting her ass.

"What's so funny?" I placed the pillows in the space her ass had just vacated.

"You. You're such a sweet talker, Jumbo."

"Yup. That's what all the girls say." I grinned at her as she lowered herself onto the pillows. "How's that feel? Comfortable?"

"Yeah, it's fine."

"Good. So let's do this. C'mon, spread 'em. Let's fuck."

Chapter 12

No doubt about it – when it came to porn, Jamie was a natural. Born to suck and fuck her way to internet fame. She was so easy to work with. Ask her to fluff up a dick or two? She got right to work. Need your balls sucked? No problem. If I asked her to bend over so I could stick a rolling pin up her ass, she'd probably respond by saying, "Oh boy, oh boy, oh boy!" So convincing her to take Joey's cumshot to her face while at the same time, down at the other end, Junior and I were plugging her pussy? Not really an issue.

"Everything okay?" I asked her as I slid my dick in and out of her cute, bald pussy at a medium speed. "You comfortable?"

"Uh-huh. I feel, … good. I love Junior, you know. He's so big."

"I think you just love dick, sweetie." I laughed and aimed my camcorder down at her cunt, capturing the action from my point of view. She was flat on her back, her ass elevated by two huge, firm pillows, her legs hanging over the end of the bed, her pussy all wet and sloppy looking and leaking so much juice it was beginning to run down to the bed. That last part – the large amount of pussy juice leaking onto my new, king-sized bed – was unfortunate. I'd ordered a half-dozen waterproof mattress pads, in six different colors, but I hadn't received them yet. They were backordered.

"Yeah, I do love dick – I'm not denying that. But Junior's special. I told you before – he's the real reason I'm here. Because the first time I saw him on Fukknumzie, … I fell in love with him. And I decided right then that Jumbo Johnson, Jr. was a dick I just had to experience stuffing my pussy and tickling my tonsils." She topped off her declaration of love for my dick with a sweet smile.

"I know how you feel," I told her as I continued jamming that dick she loved so much in and out of her cunt. "I'm kinda fond of him, too."

Joey, who'd been wandering around, shooting the action from various angles with a camcorder, interrupted Jamie's and my discussion of our mutual love for my dick. He stopped up by the head of the bed and said, "Hey, what about me? I've got a big dick, too."

Jamie leaned her head back and looked up at him. "Awww, don't feel bad, Joey. I love your dick, too."

"Sure," he said, acting as if his feelings were hurt. "That's 'cause you love *all* dicks."

She giggled. "True. But I especially love yours because it's right here, right now. Why don't you come up here on the bed and let me show you how much I love it?"

Joey looked at me for assurance that inserting himself into the scene at this time would be okay. I nodded, slowly panning my camcorder up Jamie's body in order to catch his entrance. He climbed up onto the bed, kneeling next to her head and teasing her by dangling his semi-erect dick in her face.

"Oh, wow," she said, gazing up at the large appendage that was suddenly dancing in the air above her, so close it sometimes sideswiped her nose. "Look at what just appeared. It's a miracle!" Her giggles turned into a laugh as she reached up and pulled his dick into her mouth.

A smile spread across Joey's face as Jamie pumped his dick with her hand and slurped the head. He looked at me and grinned. "Spit roasting," he said. "We're spit roasting her."

Yup, that's exactly what we were doing. We'd pierced her at both ends, just as if she was a piece of raw meat, and we were – as it's called in the porn business – *spit roasting* her. Fucking both ends of her at the same time. She seemed to be enjoying it, too.

"Warn me when you're gonna cum," I told him, watching – and videoing it, of course – as he fucked Jamie's mouth.

"Okay. It's gonna be quick. Less than 20 seconds, I'm guessing. I'm primed and ready to fire."

"Try to get it in her mouth, okay?" Joey was not known for launching his cumshots with a high degree of accuracy. His dick liked to spread his cum around, it seemed. From any distance of more than an inch or two away, he was likely to miss his target by a wide margin.

"Sure, I'll try. No guarantees, though."

"Do that," I said. "How about you, Stella? You ready?" Hey, I remembered to call her by her porn name. How about that!

"Thut, yuh, I'b beddee." She leaned her head back, getting into a better position to catch a mouthful of cum.

"Whenever you feel the urge, Joey," I told him. "Let 'er rip."

"Actually, I'm ... feeling ... the urge ... ... right *now!*" He snatched his dick out of Jamie's mouth and stroked it three times with his hand, aiming it down at her. On the third stroke, a massive cumshot came spurting out, flew across the empty space between dickhead and mouth, landed on the tip of her cute little nose, and leaked down into both nostrils. Pretty close to perfect, by Joey's standards.

Subsequent spurts weren't much better. While a couple managed to land in her mouth by accident, the rest did not. By the time Joey squeezed the last few drops of his cum into her mouth, her face was pretty much covered in sticky white fuck-juice.

"Fuck! I needed that," he said, shaking his dick one last time at Jamie's mouth. A final drop of cum flew out, landing in her left ear.

I continued slow pumping her pussy as I filmed the messy scene playing out in front of me. It may have been messy but it was going to look great in Jamie's video. I had a strong feeling – a *very* strong feeling – that Jamie had found her calling in life, her *raison d'etre*. She was born to be a cumslut. A *video* cumslut.

When Joey finally finished, his dick completely drained and a smile on his face, I tossed a towel up onto Jamie's chest so she could wipe up the parts of his cumshot that had missed her mouth and now covered significant parts of her face. But she ignored it, instead scraping cum from her cheeks and forehead with her fingers and then licking her fingers clean. She obviously hadn't been kidding when she'd told us she *loved* cum.

"Oh boy! That was ... *good!*" she said.

"My sentiments, exactly," Joey said, sitting back on his heels and watching Jamie clean herself up. "Excellent, actually."

"Yeah, excellent. Tasty. A little spicy, a little sweet. Really good." She licked her lips, discovered a tiny gob of cum she'd missed in one corner, and tongued it into her mouth. "Mmm, yum yum. Oh boy, oh boy. Did I ever tell you guys that I love cum?"

"Yeah, Jamie. I think you did," both Joey and I said at the same time.

Chapter 13

For the next two hours, Joey and I took turns fucking Jamie in every variation of missionary position we could think of and in every place in the room that lent itself to that activity. We fucked her on the bed, of course. We fucked her on the floor. We fucked her bent backward over a chair. Along the way, she threw in a plethora of orgasms in a variety of formats for her future fans to marvel at.

For a final, bring-the-curtain-down scene, *I* – just me – fucked her while she was suspended in the air, me standing and holding her up by the ass while Joey supported her upper body for me. She did manage to lean her head back and work on fluffing Joey's dick back up while we were doing that, though. No doubt about it – Jamie was going to make a *lot* of money in the porn business.

When it came time to wrap up the evening with the double cumshot I'd promised her earlier, she was more than ready. She knelt next to the bed, licking her lips and smiling up at the two of us as we stood on each side of her, jerking our dicks above her face. Joey held his camcorder in his free hand, shooting the scene looking down, POV. As usual when things were about to get messy with cum, Jamie looked eager to partake in the goings-on.

"Any second now," I announced, wailing away on Junior with my right hand. "How you doing, Joey?"

"Good. Go ahead and load her up. I'll come in right behind you."

"Okay, here we go. Open wide, Stella."

"Why bother?" Jamie said as the first spurt from my dick landed in her left eye. She blinked and added, "Isn't the whole point to cover me in cum?"

Actually, that *was* the whole point – to cover her face in cum. But I wanted to get some of it, at least, into her mouth. So after successfully coating her cheeks and forehead, plus that left eye, in creamy white goodness, I moved a little bit closer to her and laid my dick on that

61

pouty bottom lip of hers, firing the remainder of my ammunition directly onto her tongue.

"Mmmmm, good," she said, smacking her lips and swallowing. She turned her face up to Joey just as *his* cum cannon fired its first shot. Against all odds, it landed squarely in her mouth. As did shot number two.

Obviously, Joey was not aiming for her mouth because if he had been, he never would have hit it. His control over the direction of his cum flying through the air was notoriously bad – he *never* hit what he was aiming at. And for a porn actor trying to cover a girl in cum, having that cum land in her mouth instead of on her face was a problem.

Fixing that problem was easy, though. "Aim for her mouth," I told him. I knew if he did that, he'd miss by a wide margin.

It worked. Sort of. He missed her mouth. Actually, the third spurt out of Joey's dick missed Jamie completely, flying over her shoulder and landing on the rug behind her. I made a mental note to hire a part-time housekeeper, someone with a carpet-cleaning machine who could come in once a week or so and clean this place up.

Eventually, though – and probably completely by accident – he managed to land a couple of shots on her face. And one in her hair. By the time he gave his dick a final shake, we had accomplished what we'd set out to do – Jamie's face was covered in cum. She looked as if she'd been caught in a cumstorm.

She sat back on her heels and looked up at Joey's camcorder as he shot the last scene of the night – her smiling as she scraped cum off her face with her fingers, held those fingers above her head, and let the cum she'd collected drip down into her open mouth. "Yum, yum," she said. "That's delicious." Then she laughed, popped up to her feet, and trotted off in the direction of my new, spacious shower.

Yup, Jamie was a natural. No doubt about it. I hadn't told her to do any of that – she'd improvised the entire thing, all on her own.

While Jamie cleaned up in the shower, Joey and I went out into the living room and did the same things we used to do at my apartment after we'd finished our evening activities – we sat on the couch, smoked weed, drank beer, and talked. Just as a way to unwind from a tough night's work, you know. And eventually, as it usually did, our conversation got around to an appraisal of the girl we'd been working with. Jamie, in this case.

"So whaddaya think about her?" I asked him. "Like her?"

"Oh fuck yeah, I like her. What's not to like? She's fun. A real sweetheart. A complete lunatic when it comes to sex, though."

"Totally," I said, chuckling.

He tipped his beer up to his lips and took a long pull, draining the bottle. "I need another beer. You want one?" He got up and headed into the kitchen.

"I do. Bring me one, too," I called after him.

He came back with two beers, handed one over, and flopped onto the couch, next to me. "Yeah, I don't think we've ever had any girl make videos with us who liked sex as much as Jamie."

"Oh, I don't know about that," I said. "I can think of a few. She does like cum, though."

"Like it? Fuck, she *loves* it!"

"Yeah, she does, doesn't she?"

"She does what?" Jamie said, walking into the living room, drying her long blonde hair with a towel. "Are you guys talking about me?"

I added *buy a hair dryer* to my mental *things to do* list, then told her, "Yeah, we are, sweetie. We're discussing your performance, earlier."

"You were, huh? So what were you saying? What is it that I *do*?"

"Well, among other things, you suck dick like a high-priced vacuum cleaner."

"So, ... I get your dicks nice and clean. That's a good thing, right?"

"Absolutely."

"Then thank you, kind sir. I do my best." She attempted a half curtsy but ended it with a giggle when she almost fell over.

"How's your eye?" Joey asked her.

She blinked her left eye a couple of times and grinned. "I can see," she said, casting a sideways glance at me. "No thanks to Charlie."

I grinned back at her. "Sorry about that. I'll try to aim better, next time."

She leaned over and pulled the joint from my hand, took a big hit, then exhaled in the direction of my ceiling. I looked up. Unlike in my apartment, the ceiling above my couch showed no large, dark spot. I briefly wondered how long it would be until one showed up.

"I gotta get going," she said, handing the joint back to me. "So, same time next Tuesday?"

"Yup."

"What are we gonna do for our next video?"

"Pretty much the same as we did tonight, only doggy style. Joey and I are gonna fuck you silly for a couple of hours, then cum on your face."

"Sounds like fun. See you guys next week. Don't do anything I wouldn't do." She leaned over and kissed me on the cheek, then kissed Joey, laughed, and headed for the front door. When she got there she turned around, wiggled her fingers at us, said, "Toodles," laughed again, and left.

"See?" Joey said as the door closed behind her. "I was right – she's looney tunes. No girl says, 'Sounds like fun,' when you tell her you're gonna fuck her silly for hours and then cum in her face."

I took a hit off the joint and blew the smoke out toward the ceiling, again wondering about that dark spot. "You're wrong, Joey. At least one girl does. And her name is Jamie."

Chapter 14

Two days later, on Thursday morning as I was getting ready to leave for Shegley to do a little editing work, my phone rang. I didn't recognize the caller but because my number was on numerous business cards I'd given away since I'd started my career as a videographer slash porn producer, I figured it was probably a potential customer, seeking information. So I answered it.

"Hello," said a woman's pleasant-sounding voice. "Is this Mr. Charles Novak?"

"Yup. That's me. Charlie. You're talking to him. And you are?"

"I'm Judge Topin's judicial assistant. She'd like to speak with you. One moment, please."

"What?" I said, not getting an answer. I sat down on my couch and waited. After a few seconds, the voice of the pleasant-sounding woman was replaced by the sound of another woman's voice. This one did not sound as pleasant. Nor as friendly. "Mr. Novak? Mr. Charles Novak? The pornographer?"

Pornographer? Is that what I was? That sounded, ... illicit.

"I'm a videographer," I informed her.

She laughed, not sounding amused at all. "Is that what they're calling it, now?"

I remained silent, waiting to see what this was all about. Even though, since I recognized the name her secretary had provided, I had a pretty good idea. This was about Jamie.

"My name is Andrea Topin, Mr. Novak. Do you know who I am?"

"I think so. You're Jamie's mother, aren't you?"

"*Step*-mother," she corrected me.

"Sorry. Stepmother."

"Yes. Well, I'm calling to inform you that I want you to cancel her contract, refund any money she's paid you, and *stop having sex with my daughter!*"

"Stepdaughter," I said.

"What?"

"She's your stepdaughter."

"Yes. Well, that distinction is irrelevant. I want you to stop what you're doing with her. Stop making those, ... those nasty videos."

"Is that what Jamie wants?"

"That's what *I* want," she said.

"Yeah. Well, that's kinda interesting, actually. But my contract is with Jamie and she's an adult now, so it doesn't really matter what *you* want. It's up to her. Not you."

"Do you know what I do for a living, Mr. Novak?"

"Does it make a difference?"

"It might. I'm a judge. A Superior Court judge."

"Wow. Impressive," I told her. And it was, too. I was totally impressed.

"And Franklin is an attorney."

"Franklin?"

"Jamie's father."

That was impressive, as well. "Wow, a judge and an attorney. You guys must be loaded!"

"What?" she said, sounding slightly confused.

"Rich," I said. "You guys must be rich."

"That's neither here nor there, Mr. Novak. My point is, we have the ability to make your life, ... let's call it, *difficult*."

"You're threatening me?"

"No, no. Of course not. I wouldn't do that. I'm just pointing out a possible outcome if you don't do what I want. Legal action."

"Well, I'm a legal business. I have a business license. I pay my taxes. On time, too. Jamie's an adult, able to sign contracts. And I have a lawyer, too. But before we turn this into a messy public affair, with –"

"Wait. What? Why would this be messy? Or public?"

"Before I answer that, let me ask you something. You said you're a Superior Court judge, right?"

"Yes. I am."

"So, I suppose, if you're like most Superior Court judges, you'd like someday to move up to be an Appellate Court judge. Be on the Court of Appeals. Or maybe even the state Supreme Court. Right?"

"Those are possible goals for someone in my position, yes," she said, sounding extremely cautious.

"It would be a shame if a public trial, or even a hearing of some kind about this matter, resulted in extensive media coverage, don't you think? Publicity about a judge's porn star daughter could certainly hinder that judge's chances of attaining those lofty goals, it seems to me."

"Now you're threatening *me*?"

"No, no. Not at all. I'm just pointing out a possible outcome," I said, feeling *extremely* clever that I was using her own words against her.

A long period of silence followed. Finally, she said, "This isn't over, Mr. Novak. Not by a long shot. I'll be in touch." And she disconnected the call.

Huh. That was weird. Being contacted by Jamie's stepmom, I mean. I usually didn't have much contact with the parents of the girls who were my customers. Actually, this was the first time it had *ever* happened.

I reached under the couch, pulled out my stash box and took out a joint. A little weed would help me decide what I should do about this, I figured, as I fired up the joint and took a long hit. Weed always helped me to come up with creative ideas. Although, I wasn't sure I even needed a creative idea for this. It seemed to me there was a pretty good chance Judge Topin might drop this matter, convinced by my brilliant argument regarding the potential negative consequences of bad publicity on her career to just ... let it go.

Or not. After all, she was a *judge*. And Jamie's father was a lawyer. And she'd threatened me with legal action. I assumed that meant a lawsuit of some kind. Even though I felt like I hadn't done anything wrong by taking on Jamie as a client, I knew that getting sued would be costly, messy, and time consuming.

Joey should know about this, I decided. His dick had been inside Jamie almost as much as mine had. If I got sued, he probably would, too. I took a couple more hits off the joint and called him.

His girlfriend, Megan, answered his phone, saying, "Charlie! Good morning. What's up?"

"Jeez, Joey, what happened to your voice?" I said. "You sound just like a girl."

She laughed. "Joey's in the shower. So how's my second favorite porn actor these days?"

"Pretty good. How's business? You still making lots of money?" Megan was a Fukknumzie girl, performing as Bonnie, the Butt-Fuck Queen of the West, and was one of that website's more successful *entrepreneurs*.

"Fuck, Charlie, I am making *so* much money. It's unbelievable!"

"Good for you, sweetie. I'm glad." Actually, I already knew that Megan was making a bundle from her videos. Joey had told me. "So when are you gonna come visit the new studio, anyway?"

"Soon. I really want to see it. I'm gonna come over one of these nights with Joey to check it out and watch you guys work out one of the girls."

"Come next Tuesday. You'll get to see a girl who's gonna be the next big thing. Jamie."

"Oh, yeah. Joey told me about her. He said she's crazy."

"She's not crazy. She just likes dick. She really, really, *really* likes dick."

"Well, that's a good thing if you wanna be a success in this business. Right?"

"Yup. It is. Actually, she's the reason I called. Something's come up with her and I need to talk to Joey about it."

"Okay. Sure. I'll have him call you when he gets out of the shower."

"Perfect. You be good, now," I told her, preparing to hang up.

"Good's not good enough," Charlie. "I wanna be *great!*"

"Be good is just an expression, Meg. You're already great." I laughed and disconnected, then sat back, sucked more smoke into my lungs, and waited for Joey to call me back.

Chapter 15

On Thursday, when I'd first heard from her, Judge Topin had told me she'd 'be in touch.' At the time, I'd assumed that meant more phone calls. Probably from a lawyer. Maybe Jamie's dad. So when I answered the door and saw the attractive, middle-aged woman standing there at one o'clock on the following Monday afternoon, I was surprised. Somehow, without ever having seen her before, I knew I was looking at Jamie's mother. Excuse me – *stepmother*.

"Mr. Novak?" she said.

"Charlie. My friends call me Charlie."

"We're not friends, Mr. Novak. I'm Andrea Topin, Jamie's stepmother. The *judge*." That last word came out sounding like a threat.

"Well, I'm still Charlie."

"May I come in?"

"Sure." I held the door wide and stood aside.

"Have a seat," I told her when we ended up in the living room.

She sat down on the couch, glancing around the room. "This isn't exactly what I expected," she said.

"No? What did you expect? Beds with naked women on them?"

"Not that, no. But this, ... this looks just like ... a living room."

"Because that's what it is."

"I thought this was where you made your videos."

"No, we have a studio for that. In Shegley." I said, conveniently forgetting to include the fact that until this week, this *was* where Joey, myself, and dozens of girls had made videos. Porn videos. Right here in my apartment.

"I see," she said.

I thought about asking her if she wanted to share a joint with me but decided she probably wouldn't be up for that. Being a judge and all, you know. "So, what can I do for you, today? I suppose this is about Jamie."

"It is. I thought perhaps if we talked – in person – I could convince you to cancel her contract."

"Uh-huh. Okay, well, I'll listen to what you have to say, even though I've already told you what my position is. But before you ... lay out your case, I'm gonna get a beer. You want one?"

"Are they cold?"

"Of course they're cold. Who drinks warm beer, anyway?"

"The British."

"I'm American," I said. "So, you want one or not?"

"Fine. If you're going to have one, I'll have one, too."

I went into the kitchen, grabbed two beers from the fridge – checking to make sure they were nice and cold – and went back to the living room, handing one to her and then sitting down beside her.

"No glass?" Her eyebrows lifted, as if I'd offended her by offering her beer straight from the bottle.

"No glass," I said.

"I suppose that's all right." She tipped the bottle up to her lips and very delicately took three small sips, one right after another.

I took a drink of my own beer and checked her out. She definitely wasn't what I'd envisioned when I'd found out she was a judge. I'd pictured her as being in her 50s, several pounds overweight, with wrinkles, graying hair pulled back in a bun, bifocals, and a stern expression that was a permanent feature of her face. Instead, she was tall and slender, with medium-long, curly blonde hair and intense, piercing blue eyes. And she definitely wasn't in her 50s. If anything, she looked closer to 30, even though I knew she had to be older than that. Jamie had told me she'd been her stepmother since she was a little girl, and Jamie was 18. Whatever her age, Jamie's stepmom was *hot!* A MILF!

Neither one of us spoke for a while, until eventually the judge looked at me and said, "I must say, I'm surprised, Mr. Novak."

"Surprised about what?"

"You."

"Me? What's surprising about me?"

"You're not what I expected."

"No? What did you expect?"

"Some kind of superhero, I guess." She took another three small sips of her beer and wiped her mouth with the back of her hand. Then, perhaps having second thoughts about the amount of beer she was consuming, she brought the bottle back up to her lips and chugged about half its contents. I waited for her to burp but she didn't.

"A superhero, huh?" I chuckled. "What made you think that?"

"Jamie. She talks about you like you're some kind of Greek god, always telling me how big you are, how powerful. I thought you'd be, ... taller, more muscular, have lots of tattoos, maybe be wearing a loincloth or something like that."

My chuckles turned into a laugh. So that's how Judge Topin knew what Jamie had been doing on Tuesday nights – evidently, Jamie had told her. "Sorry to disappoint you," I said.

"I didn't say I was disappointed. Just surprised." She drained the rest of her beer and offered me the empty bottle, saying, "Can I get another?"

"Sure." I took her empty and left to fetch two more beers.

"I really thought you'd be a lot bigger," she said when I returned. "To hear Jamie tell it, you're not just big, you're *huge*. And *thick*. Like a bodybuilder or something. That's what I was expecting you to be – big and thick. But you're not. You're just, ... normal size." She took a big drink of her fresh beer and smacked her lips.

"Well, ..."

"Well, what?"

"You might have misunderstood what Jamie meant," I said. "I don't think she was talking about my body."

"Really? What, then?"

"Uh, I think when she said I was huge and, uh, thick, she meant, ... uh, ..."

"Yes?"

"My dick."

Her eyebrows rose. "What?"

"My penis, I mean."

"I know what a dick is, Mr. Novak. I'm not a prude." She finished her beer and I got her another one. When I came back, she said, "So it's your *dick* that's big? And thick? That's what Jamie has been talking about?"

"Yup." I nodded.

"I see." She took another long swallow of beer. "How big is it?"

"Pretty big."

"*How* big?"

I held up my hands, about a foot apart.

"Your kidding, right?" she said.

"Nope."

"It's really that long?"

"Yup."

"And thick, too?"

"Yup. Extra thick, actually."

"I don't think I believe you."

There wasn't much I could do about that. I shrugged. "You think Jamie's been lying to you?"

"No, ... she's just exaggerating, probably."

"She's not," I said.

She sat there, nodding her head as if she was responding to some internal dialogue, and staring at me. Finally, she said, "Can I see it?"

I was certain I must have misunderstood what she'd said. "What?"

"Your dick. I want to see what it looks like. Can you show it to me?"

"Really? You want me to show you my dick?"

"I'm a judge, Mr. Novak. I can't just take your word for it that you have a gigantic dick. I need to see the evidence. Show me your penis."

Putting my beer on the coffee table, I stood up in front of her. "You're sure?" I said.

"I'm sure."

I dropped my shorts.

"Oh, my," she said, glancing back and forth between my face and my dick. "It *is* big. Not as big as you said, though."

"Yup. Right now, when he's kinda relaxed and everything, he's at about half size."

"So, ... it gets bigger when you, ... when you get aroused?"

"When I get a hard-on, yup. Doubles in size."

"I'd like to see that," she said, licking her lips. "I'd really, *really* like to see that."

Chapter 16

The amount of elapsed time between Judge Topin saying she'd like to see my dick in its *performing* shape and her ending up on the floor, between my legs, was approximately three seconds. Add another few seconds to that for a quick handjob – just to make sure Junior was as large and as firm as possible, probably – and I found my dick captured by the warm, wet suction of her mouth. So, ... a total of about 10 seconds, then.

"Uh, Mrs. Topin? Judge? What are you doing?" I said as I watched her enthusiastically slurping away on my dick.

She pulled Junior out of her mouth and fixed me with a *what-are-you-stupid?* look. "What does it look like I'm doing, Mr. Novak?"

"Well, ... it, uh, ... it looks like you're kneeling between my legs and sucking my dick."

"Exactly. Is that a problem?"

"Not really. Just one thing, though."

"What?" She sounded impatient.

"Can you call me Charlie? Mr. Novak sounds like my father."

"Fine. *Charlie.* There – are you happy now?"

"Um, ... almost. I think if you go back to what you were doing, that would make me happy."

For the first time since I'd met her, she smiled. "I'm not going to suck your giant dick until you cum, you know."

"You're not?"

"No, I'm – what is it you pornographers call it? Fluffing? Yes, that's it. That's what I'm doing. I'm *fluffing* your dick."

"Why?"

"To make it hard, of course."

"He's pretty hard, already," I informed her. That was true. Just two or three licks from the judge's tongue had changed Junior from a *limpy* into a *stiffy*.

"And to make it as big as possible, too."

"You're kidding, right? Look. He's already *huge*."

"I know. Very impressive, actually. And I understand now why Jamie said she was in love with it. It's a remarkable piece of male architecture. But I need it to be in tip-top shape."

"Why?" I said, although I already had a pretty good idea what the answer to my question was.

"Because I'm going to do to you what you've been doing to my stepdaughter."

"You mean ...?"

"Yes. That's exactly what I mean, *Charlie*. I intend to fuck you silly. But first, I want to make sure this fat piece of meat here is just as *fluffy* as I can make it." She gobbled Junior back into her mouth, licked his head a few times, then attempted to swallow him.

Good luck with that deep throat stuff, Judge, I thought. *Many have tried. All have failed.*

As Jamie's stepmom practiced her head bobbing technique on my dick, I reached over and picked up the remote control for the big camera that sat silently staring at us from down at the end of the couch. Since all I really needed here at my apartment was one camcorder for auditions, I'd been planning to move that big camera out to the new studio in Shegley but hadn't gotten around to it yet. As I pushed the button to turn it on, I was glad I hadn't. Having video proof of my encounter with Judge Topin somehow seemed like an excellent idea.

I watched her work for a while. She tried, over and over, to throat Junior right down to my pubes, but didn't have much success. Each time, as her mouth slid a little bit past halfway down my shaft, she gagged, then ended up pulling her mouth off my dick, gasping for air. Still felt pretty good, though. At least, to me.

"You wanna go see my bedroom?" I asked her.

"What for?" she said, looking up at me as she rested her throat.

"Big bed. Plenty of room for you to fuck me silly."

She hesitated briefly, as if she might be having second thoughts about that whole *fuck me silly* plan of hers, then said, "All right. Let's go."

I led her down the hall toward my bedroom, feeling a little uncomfortable about the situation in which I now found myself. Sure, I wanted to fuck her – she was hot. Extremely fuckable. And thanks to that hot, juicy mouth of hers, Junior was all pumped up and raring to show her a good time.

But this was Jamie's stepmother. She was a judge. And all I was wearing was a T-shirt. I was naked from the waist down. And Judge Topin had her hand on my bare ass. Just about any guy finding himself in this position – experienced porn actor or not – would find it to be awkward.

* * *

I had to cancel my Monday evening session. Muffin, the girl who was scheduled to enjoy my dick and my knowledge of how to use it, was slightly upset when I called and told her, but I had no choice – I was fucked out! Andrea, as I was now allowed to call Jamie's stepmom, had done a number on Junior, draining him twice in quick succession. There was no way I could give Muffin the good fucking she deserved.

Yup, at least for the time being, Junior was dead. Well, not really *dead*, of course. Just temporarily out of commission. Like, ... in a coma. And for that, I had Andrea to thank. Or to blame, I guess.

I'd never fucked a MILF before. Or a judge, either, for that matter. Nearly all the girls I'd been fucking were in their 20s. And while I certainly enjoyed the fresh taste and the tightness of young pussies, fucking Andrea had shown me there was a lot to be said for experience, too.

I'd fucked her – wait, scratch that, *she'd* fucked *me* in about a dozen different positions and managed to extract two gigantic loads of cum from the always-eager-to-please Junior. Her pussy was tight and juicy and her skill at using it was unparalleled. Junior never stood a chance.

And she'd accomplished all this in less than an hour because she had to be back in court by three o'clock. Very impressive, in my opinion. Heck, she was even in the process of slurping that limp excuse for a functioning dick, trying to get him enthused about more dick-in-pussy action, when she noticed the time and decided she needed to leave.

I didn't even get up when she left. Not enough energy. I just stretched out on my big, soft bed and watched her get dressed, give both me and Junior a quick kiss, and tell us she'd "be in touch." I was still lying there, wondering what she'd meant – in touch about the Jamie situation or in touch because she wanted to play with Junior some more – when I fell asleep.

Chapter 17

"You fucked her mother?" Joey said. His face showed a combination of shocking surprise and respect. "Jamie's mother? Really?"

"Her stepmother," I corrected him.

He shook his head. "Not cool, dude."

"Well, in my defense, technically, I didn't fuck *her* – she fucked *me*. Twice."

It was the day after my unannounced visit from Judge Topin – Andrea, as I now liked to think of her. Joey and I were sitting on the couch in the new studio, smoking weed and drinking beer while we waited for Jamie to show up for her Tuesday night session. Joey, as he frequently did, had shown up early. He was serious about his work as a dick for hire and was always eager to get started.

"You gonna tell her?"

I chugged a giant swallow of beer as I watched him bogart the joint. "That I fucked her stepmom?"

"Yeah."

"I'm not sure. What do you think? Should I?"

"Fuck, no, you shouldn't. Why would you? It doesn't affect what she's doing here, does it?" He hit the joint for the fourth time in a row – I counted them – and finally passed it over to me.

"I don't know. It might." I took the final hit and tossed the roach into the ashtray.

The front door opened and Jamie came bouncing into the room, smiling and humming tunelessly. She crossed the room and stood in front of the couch, looking hot as hell in super-short shorts and an old, white T-shirt that was so thin I could see her nipples. "Hi guys. Ready for a big night of sucking and fucking?" she said with a giggle.

"See?" Joey said, turning to look at me. "I told you. Listen to her. Sucking and fucking – that's all she thinks about. She's crazy."

She poked him with her foot – a fake kick to the shin – and grinned at him. "I'm not crazy. I just like dick the same way you and Charlie like pussy. Maybe I'm a little oversexed for a girl but I'm not crazy."

"A *little* oversexed?"

She kicked him again – a little harder, a little less fake, this time. "Fuck you, Joey. You better be careful what you say or you'll be watching from the sidelines, tonight."

Joey acted properly chagrined. "Sorry, sweetheart. I was just teasing. You know I love fucking that cute, tight little pussy of yours. And I love your enthusiasm, too. You really know how to drain a dick."

She giggled again. "I do, don't I? I really do!"

"You certainly do," he said. I nodded my agreement.

"I'm gonna get a beer," she said, heading for the kitchen.

"Bring a couple for us, too," I called after her.

"So," Jamie said, once she was back with the beers and comfortably seated between us. "What are we gonna do tonight?"

"Well, normally we concentrate on doggy style for the second video." I pulled out a fresh joint, fired it up and handed it to her, watching as she sucked smoke into her lungs. Underneath that thin white T-shirt she was wearing, her tits seemed to get bigger.

"*Concentrate* on doggy style? What's that mean, exactly?"

"It means it doesn't make any difference what position we're featuring in a video, there's always some other stuff, too, you know. Foreplay. Some dick sucking, a little pussy eating, things like that. Maybe even some quick fucking in other positions. But we *concentrate* on the main position."

"I see."

"You know, we can do whatever you want. They're your videos. You're in charge. Just remember, though – if you want your videos to sell, you have to give people what they want to see."

She took a sip of her beer and looked thoughtful. "You know what I'd like to see?"

"What?"

"More pussy eating."

"Yeah?"

"Yeah. There's like a gazillion videos of girls sucking dicks. They're everywhere – easy to find. But trying to find a good pussy-eating video is next to impossible."

"Actually, I've noticed that, too. Not a lot of cunt-munching videos on Fukknumzie." I took a sip of my beer and watched Jamie sucking on the joint, not passing it to either Joey or me.

"So let's make one, then," she said. "A whole video of nothing but tongue work."

"You don't wanna do the doggy-fuck video?"

"Hmm, ... well, that sounds good, too. Maybe we could just throw a little bit of that in at the end, just before the big, final cumshots. Whaddaya think?"

"Hey, you're the boss. Whatever you want us to do, we'll do it."

"Okay, good. That's the way I wanna do it, then." She paused to take a drink of her beer. "You'll do anything, huh?"

"Just about."

"Even rimming? I never see that in any of your videos."

"Rimming?"

"Yeah. Eating ass."

I chuckled. "I know what it is, Jamie. You like that, do you? Getting your asshole tongued?"

"Fuck, yes. It feels great. I never let guys fuck me in the ass unless they're willing to loosen up my asshole with their tongues first," she said. Then she slapped her hand over her mouth and giggled. "Whoops! I mean ... I *wouldn't* let guys do that to me unless they were willing to tongue my asshole."

"Of course not," I said.

Joey grinned and shook his head. "Fuck, Jamie, you're really nasty. You know that?"

"Oh, yeah? And like you guys aren't? You guys are way nastier than me."

She had a point, there. Nasty was kind of our business. We specialized in nasty.

"Lemme see if I've got this straight. In addition to eating your pussy, you want us to eat your ass, too? Is that it?"

"Yeah, I guess so. What else is there to eat down there?" she said, giggling. She took a final hit off the joint and tossed it in the ashtray. She'd smoked the entire thing by herself – Joey and I hadn't had even one hit. "So, do you that? Rim jobs?"

"If we like the girl enough, we do," I told her.

"So, ... what about me? Do you like *me* enough?" she asked, casting a hopeful look in my direction.

"Oh, yeah, Jamie. We definitely like you. We like you a whole fucking bunch. And we'd be more than happy to eat your ass." I looked over at Joey. "Right, Joey?"

"Absolutely," he said, licking his lips and nodding his head. "Abso-fucking-lutely!"

Chapter 18

Joey and I spent almost the entirety of Jamie's session with our heads between Jamie's legs, eating her pussy and tonguing her asshole. Tonguing it, of course, because you can't really *eat* ass in the same way you eat pussy. You can't *really* get your whole face in there and just shake it back and forth like a mad dog as you slobber all over it with your lips and tongue and even your nose, like you can with a cunt. There's not enough room. Not enough *stuff* to work with. And butt cheeks get in the way.

Actually, that's not entirely true. There *are* way to do what I just described. It was just that Jamie had a favorite position for getting rimmed – elbows and knees, ass high in the air. And that made eating her ass slightly difficult. If I had to guess, she preferred being posed like that because it was easy to slip from rimming right into buttfucking. Doggy style – that's the way most girls prefer to take a dick up their ass.

But we didn't do any of that. Fuck Jamie in the ass, I mean. We were saving that for her very last video, so she could fast for a day or so beforehand. That was something we recommended to all our clients – don't eat a lot the day before you're going to get fucked in the ass.

Anyway, we didn't have time for buttfucking. We managed to fit in some *vagina-style* dog fucking and a double cumshot at the end of the evening, then called it quits. It was almost midnight. We were tired. And all three of us were exhibiting other signs indicating we should stop for the night, as well.

Jamie's pussy was a bright pink, her asshole was a bright pink, and her face, ... well, her face wasn't pink. It didn't have those mild friction burns from too much licking, the way those other parts of her body did. Her face was just happy. She was smiling.

Joey and I, though, were keeping *our* smiles to a minimum – we both were suffering from *tired tongue and jaw syndrome*, a rare but temporary – thankfully – affliction. And Joey's face was pink. Red, actually. *Bright* red.

"What?" he said when he noticed me staring at him. We were sitting on the couch, indulging in our usual after-session activities – drinking beer and smoking weed. The perfect way to end an evening.

"How're you gonna explain about your face to Megan?" I asked him.

"What's wrong with my face?"

"It's red. From your nose down – bright red."

He laughed, almost choking on the beer he was in the process of drinking.

I waited until he recovered and said, "What's so funny?"

"I wasn't going to say anything but, ... so's yours!" He laughed again. "Red as a cucumber."

"Cucumbers aren't red, Joey."

"I meant tomato. Red as a tomato."

"Whatever. I don't have a live-in girlfriend I have to go home to. And explain the friction burns on my face to."

"Meg probably won't even notice. She knows I eat pussy on the job."

"Yeah, but does she know you eat ass?"

He shrugged. "Probably. She knows I eat *hers*."

I was still laughing when Jamie came back from her shower.

"What?" she said. "What's so funny? What did I miss?"

"Nothing," I said. "We were just laughing about the way our faces look."

"Aww, you guys look cute. Red is definitely your color – both of you."

"Thanks, I think. Get a beer and join us," I told her.

"Sure. I'm gonna just call for an Uber, first. It usually takes them a while to get out here to Shegley."

"Save your money, Jamie," Joey said. "I'll give you a ride home."

"Yeah?"

"Sure. It's on my way."

"Okay, great. Lemme get that beer, then."

* * *

After Joey and Jamie left, I decided I was too tired to drive the eight miles to my apartment, so I spent the night sleeping on the couch at the studio and went home in the morning, stopping along the way to pick up a gourmet breakfast to take with me – two Egg McMuffins, hotcakes, hash browns, and a large, *very* hot coffee. In spite of the injection of caffeine, I felt sleepy after I ate, so I decided to take a short nap.

I went into my bedroom and crashed on top of my bed. I was just starting to nod off, still drifting between wakefulness and sleep, when a loud, clanging sound jolted me back to full consciousness. Someone was frantically ringing my doorbell.

I threw on a pair of shorts, rubbed my eyes and smoothed my hair as best as I could, and went to answer the door. Still half asleep, I opened it and blinked out into the sunlight. A familiar face slowly filtered its way into my vision.

"Jamie? What are you doing here?"

"I need to talk to you," she said, brushing past me into the apartment. As she did, she gave me a funny look. "Were you sleeping?"

"Yeah. I was taking a nap." I closed the door and followed her into the living room.

"Shame on you. You're supposed to be working." She sat down on the couch and crossed her ankles.

I stared at her, blinking several times to get my eyes to focus correctly. Dressed in a blue, pleated skirt and a white blouse, she looked every bit like the high school student she actually was. "Well, I was tired. You wore me out last night," I explained.

She smiled. But at the same time, she looked nervous.

"So, ... you wanted to talk to me? About what?"

"My stepmother."

"Andrea?"

"What? You know her?"

"Uh, ..."

"You called her by her first name. You know her, don't you?"

"Yeah, we've met. She dropped by a few days ago and introduced herself." The little voice in my head, Pete, laughed and said, *Yeah, that was some introduction!*

"She did? Why?" Jamie said.

"To try and convince me to drop you as a client. She doesn't want you to be a Fukknumzie girl."

"I know. She's been hassling me so much about what I'm doing, about making the videos. She grumbles about it all the time. And I'm sick of it. That's the reason I'm here, you know."

A sudden wave of disappointment swept over me. "So, ... what? You're gonna quit?"

"Quit? Fuck no, I'm not gonna quit."

"I don't understand. Then why are you here? Why don't you explain that to me?"

"Well, like I said, I got tired of tired of her constant nagging."

"Uh-huh. And?"

"And I ran away from home." Her shoulders slumped, as if to admit she knew that hadn't been the smartest play she could have made.

"What?"

"Yeah. And, well, now I'm kinda like, ... homeless. I need a place to stay. I'd stay with my dad but he's just as bad as Andrea, you know – always nagging me about stuff I wanna do. Soooo, ... I was hoping you'd let me stay here with you, Charlie."

Chapter 19

Bad idea! Bad idea! Bad, bad, bad idea, warned the little voice in my head.

She'd run away from home? And she wanted to stay here? With me? Whatever I'd expected Jamie to say when I asked her why she'd showed up at my apartment, that was definitely not it. "Jamie, you can't run away from home," I told her.

"Sure I can. I already did. And now I need someplace to stay. It'll only be temporary, Charlie. Just for a couple of days, honest. Then I'll go back home and Andrea will be so glad to have me back she'll quit bugging me."

"No, that's not what I mean. You can't run away from home because you're an adult. And adults are free to come and go as they please. You can leave any time you want."

She huffed out a short laugh. "Yeah, try telling that to a stepmother who's a judge!"

Yeah, I could see where that might make things difficult. I considered her request. I knew letting her stay with me was a bad idea. That even though it sounded as if it might be fun, living with a beautiful young girl who was basically a sex fiend, who liked nothing better than playing suck and fuck games, would lead to ... complications. Would disrupt my schedule. Would probably totally fuck up my life. Especially if her stepmother found out – just when I thought I'd solved that problem. "Well, ..." I said.

"Please, Charlie. Puh-leeze. " She offered me a sweet, nervous, hopeful smile.

Fuck! There I was – stuck between the proverbial rock and a hard place. What was I supposed to do, anyway? "Two days?"

"Three at the most. I promise I'll be good. I'll stay out of your hair, won't bother you at all."

"Uh-huh." I gave her a disbelieving look.

"I will! You won't even know I'm here."

I doubted that. "Well, ..."

"Please, Charlie. Pretty please, with sugar on top." She put her hands together in the universal prayer position, trying her best to look like a young girl at church. And doing a helluva good job of it, too.

"Yeah, I suppose you can stay with me. But just for a couple of days, okay?"

She bounced up and down a couple of times and clapped her prayer hands together, then leaned over and hugged me. "Thank you, Charlie. Thank you, thank you, thank you!" And then, to seal the deal, I guess, she kissed me.

That voice in my head – Paranoid Pete, as I'd named him, long ago, for some inexplicable reason – laughed again and said, *Worst decision of your life, Charles. You. Are. Fucked!*

I hated to admit it to myself but, deep down, I thought Pete was right. This likely *was* the worst decision I'd made in a long, long time. And though I wasn't fucked yet, with Jamie hanging around, I no doubt soon would be.

"So, what are you planning to do, today?" she said.

"Do? Well, right now, I'm planning to go back to bed. I didn't get enough sleep last night. So make yourself at home. Help yourself to anything."

"Yeah, okay. And thanks again," she said to my back as I headed down the hall.

Closing the bedroom door behind me, I tossed my shorts onto a chair and flopped onto my bed. I knew I was being rude, just storming off and leaving her sitting there alone on the couch but, fuck, I'd been blindsided. Gobsmacked. Her request had caught me totally by surprise. This was *not* how I'd been expecting to spend my Wednesday morning. I lay there, staring at the ceiling, wondering if agreeing to let Jamie stay with me was the worst idea I'd ever had or the best.

Less than five minutes later, I heard my bedroom door quietly open. In the dim light, I saw Jamie come in and start stripping off her clothes. All of them. Every last stitch.

"What are you doing, Jamie?"

"It's starting to rain. Hard. It's pounding on the roof."

"Uh-huh. I heard it."

"The sound of rain makes me sleepy."

"So?"

"I decided I need a nap, too. So I'm taking off my clothes. I don't want to sleep in them and get them all wrinkled." She crawled up onto the bed and snuggled up next to me. Then she scooted down just a bit, rested her head against the side of my chest, and draped her arm across me. "Mmm, I like this. This is really cozy. Nighty night," she said.

Fuck! What was wrong with this girl? Did she really think I was going to be able to fall asleep with a naked girl in my bed? Half on top of me? Hugging me? While I was naked, too? I began to think Joey was right. Jamie *was* crazy.

My dick – Junior – began to inflate. Slowly harden. And lengthen. Thicken. It was inevitable, I guess, what with him being down there so close to Jamie's pussy. Once Junior caught a whiff of nearby pussy, turning into a hard-on was his normal reaction.

Jamie giggled.

"What?" I said, even though I knew why she'd done that, or thought I did. Junior, in his search for the source of the aromatic pussy scent that had caught his attention, had accidentally brushed against her.

"Something poked me."

"Hmm, I wonder what it could have been."

I felt the arm that had been draped across me move, sliding down my body. The hand at the end of that arm searched for and found Junior, then wrapped around him. "You're horny?" she said, sliding her hand back and forth and sounding surprised.

"Yeah. Having a naked girl lying on top of me makes me horny," I admitted.

"Want me to smooch Junior for you?"

"Smooch him?"

"You know. Drain him." She smacked her lips, making kissing sounds. "Like that. It'll help you sleep."

"Hmm," I said. An interesting question. Should I let Jamie suck me off? Or not? It would definitely give me the drowsies, help me to fall asleep. That would be good. But knowing Jamie, she probably wouldn't be happy with simply giving me a blowjob. She'd likely want me to do something in return, like eat her out or just gift her with a good fucking. Then one thing would lead to another and we'd end up spending the entire day in bed, playing with each other's genitals.

And while spending the day playing with each other's junk *sounded* like a good thing, it actually wasn't. My Wednesday night session with Teresa, coming up in just a few hours, would be ruined if Junior couldn't perform because Jamie had already sucked him dry for the day.

Decisions, decisions. What to do, what to do. Should I let Jamie *smooch* my dick or not? However, before I could make up my mind, she made the decision for me. She slid down and slurped Junior into her mouth.

"Mmm," I said, as she ran her tongue up the bottom of my shaft, stopping to concentrate on the underside of my dickhead. The sweet spot. My body jerked and I moaned.

"Want me to stop?" she said, spitting Junior out into her hand and gazing up at me.

"Fuck, no, Jamie. Don't stop. Keep smooching!"

Giving me a lecherous grin, she returned to her *smooching* duties.

And while I still didn't know whether letting Jamie stay with me would turn out to be a good idea or not, one thing was pretty clear. What she was doing down there with my dick in her mouth *was* a good idea. In fact, it was excellent.

Chapter 20

Jamie was an amazing bed partner. By noon, when we took a lunch break, she'd already sucked me off twice and I'd munched her pussy to one gigantic, flop-around-the-bed orgasm and a couple of minor ones, as well. And I was happy I'd decided to let her stay.

I ordered some food and while we waited for it to be delivered, we sat on the couch, smoking and drinking beer. Although we had gotten dressed, Jamie had managed to unzip my fly and had her left hand in my shorts, her fingers wrapped around a limp Junior, forcing her to use only her right hand to smoke and drink. She didn't seem to mind.

No fucking had been involved. Yet. But since it was still raining, there was no doubt in my mind we'd be heading back to bed after lunch and my dick would be pounding her cunt before long. It was inevitable. And I was looking forward to it.

I nodded down at her hand. "Why do you do like to do that, anyway?" I asked her.

"Like to do what?" She took a sip of her beer.

"Hold my limp dick in your hand."

She glanced down at her hand, looking slightly surprised, as if she hadn't realized what she'd been doing. "Oh. Well, I don't want him to get lonely, you know. Think that I've abandoned him or something."

Yup. She was definitely crazy. "Dicks can't *think*, Jamie. About anything."

"I'm not so sure. It seems like they do." She gave Junior a squeeze, getting a slight – *very* slight – reaction. "See? I squeezed Junior and he answered me back."

"Yeah? What did he say?"

She grinned at me. "He said he likes it when I squeeze him and he *really* likes it when I smooch him and he hopes I'll do it a lot more."

"He said all that, huh?"

"Yup. Watch what happens." She yanked Junior out of my shorts and stood him up tall in front of me. Tall, ... but still limp. She attempted a couple of hand slides but, as you probably know, sliding your hand back and forth on a limp dick is just about impossible, so she quickly gave up on that. Instead, she leaned down and apparently was about to suck him into her mouth and somehow prove to me that dicks could think. Unfortunately, she was interrupted when the doorbell rang, announcing the arrival of our lunch.

"Fuck!" she said, glancing up toward the door. "Bad timing."

I pulled Junior away from Jamie's greedy mouth, hopped off the couch, and stuffed him back into my shorts. "Time to eat," I said.

"I was *gonna* eat," she said.

I laughed and left to get our lunch.

* * *

"You want more fries?" I said.

Jamie burped. "Yeah, maybe one more," she said, taking a handful.

I scooped up the hamburger wrappers and used napkins from the coffee table, grabbed a couple more fries for myself, and took our lunch leftovers into the kitchen, depositing it all in the garbage container under my sink. The rain was still coming down – hard, too – and it didn't look as if it would be clearing up anytime soon. The entire area was socked in. Nothing but gray skies and dark, low-hanging clouds, lending a gloomy and depressing aura to everything around.

"Thanks for lunch, Charlie," she told me when I came back and joined her on the couch.

"No problem."

She reached over and rubbed her hand on the inside of my thigh. "I'm so glad you turned out to be a nice guy, you know."

I snorted. "Nice guy? Fuck, Jamie, I am not nice."

"Sure you are. You hardly know me and yet you let me stay here with you and you bought me lunch and you –"

"You know why I'm in this business? Why I make porn videos? It's because I love pussy. I do this because it's an easy way to score a lot of pussy."

"So? That doesn't make you not nice. You love pussy. Big deal. You're a guy – guys love pussy. It's a fact. You know, I love dick – a lot, actually – and I think *I'm* still a nice person."

Wow. Jamie loves dick. There's a surprise. "You *are* nice, Jamie. You're a sweet girl and I like you a lot."

"Really?"

I nodded. Emphatically. "Really."

She leaned over and wrapped her arms around me, gave me a hug and kissed me on the cheek. "I like you, too, Charlie. And you *are* nice."

"Thanks, sweetie," I said, returning her hug.

"So, you wanna go back to bed? This is sleeping weather, you know."

"Yeah, I do. Just lemme send a couple of texts, first. Let Teresa – that's the girl I'm supposed to be working with tonight – and Joey know that I'm canceling tonight's session."

"Teresa?"

"Yup. You know her?"

"No. Is she pretty?"

"Uh, she's *cute*. Really cute."

"Cuter than me?"

I grinned at her but didn't say anything. I wasn't about to answer that. Mama didn't raise no fool.

She smiled back at me and punched me in the arm. More of a push with a closed hand, actually. "C'mon, Charlie, tell me. Is she better looking than me?"

I reached out and locked my arms around her, toppling both of us over and making her squeal. "No one I know is better looking than you, Jamie. Honestly, you're one of the most gorgeous girls I've ever seen in my entire life."

"I'll bet you say that to all the girls," she said, smiling up at me. "See? You're nice."

Maybe I did say stuff like that to all the girls, but it wasn't exactly a snow job. And I wasn't doing it to be *nice*, either. All of them *were* pretty good looking, and letting them know I thought so was a confidence builder, helping them to believe they were doing the right thing and that their good looks were going to make them a lot of money on Fukknumzie.

"Lemme send those texts," I said, pulling her back upright and grabbing my phone off the coffee table.

"Whaddaya gonna say? What's gonna be your excuse?"

"Oh, it's this cold I'm coming down with. Sneezing. Runny nose, too. Wouldn't want anyone else to catch it, you know."

She nodded. "That's good. They'll believe that. Especially with this weather."

I sent the texts and we headed into the bedroom to resume our *nap*, although I wasn't really expecting to get much sleep.

Chapter 21

The weather continued to suck. Well, that wasn't entirely true – we needed the rain. Badly. I just wasn't crazy about it because days of rainy weather had made me lazy. Sleepy. All I wanted to do was stay in bed.

Jamie had a lot to do with that, I suppose. Although she was supposed to stay with me for only a 'couple of days,' she was still in my bed when Saturday morning dawned, still raining. Neither of us had mentioned that she was supposed to be gone, probably because we were having so much fun in the bedroom.

Jamie's mouth was a face-fucker's dream – she constantly had my dick in her mouth, slurping it and licking it whether it was as hard as a rock or as limp as a boiled noodle. She must have sucked me off more than a dozen times during the three days we'd spent in bed. My dick was sore from overuse and I'd accomplished nothing during that time other than sending texts to cancel my evening appointments and giving Jamie about five times as many orgasms as she'd given me. But as for any work-related items, like editing – absolutely nothing.

At about 10 Saturday morning, as I lay on my back while Jamie sat on my dick, riding me like I was a horse, my phone buzzed. I picked it up from the nightstand and although I didn't recognize the number, it seemed vaguely familiar. Jamie was making a lot of noise, moaning and swearing as she prepared to cum for about the gazillionth time, so I put my index finger to my lips and shushed her, saying, "I'm gonna take this." She came to a complete stop and leaned forward, resting on top of me and watching quietly as I answered the call.

"Hello, Mr. Novak," said a familiar-sounding voice when I answered.

"It's Charlie, Andrea." I put my phone on speaker so Jamie could hear what her stepmother had to say.

"Yes. Well, good morning. I hope I'm not disturbing you."

"Not at all," I lied. More like a small fib, really – I couldn't very well tell her what I was doing. Jamie wiggled her hips, teasing Junior, and grinned at me. "What can I do for you?" I said.

"Have you seen Jamie recently?"

"I saw her Tuesday evening. Is something wrong?"

"Not since then?" she said, ignoring my question.

"Actually, I've been sick with a cold for the last several days and I haven't been going out."

"I'm sorry to hear that. So, you haven't seen her since then?"

This time, I ignored *her* question. "Did something happen to Jamie? Is she all right?" I asked her.

"I'm not sure. I hope so."

"What happened?"

"Oh, we had an argument. About you, actually. And her, too, of course. About what the two of you have been doing, making those videos. And she left."

"Left?"

"Yes, on Wednesday. She walked out of the house and I haven't seen her since. I'd assumed she went to stay with her father – she does that, sometimes, when we argue – but I talked to him a little while ago and he hasn't seen her or heard from her recently."

"I see."

"I'm worried about her, Charles. We can't find her."

I never could get her to call me Charlie on a consistent basis. I suppose *Charles* was better than her calling me Mr. Novak, though. After all, I'd had my dick in her mouth *and* her cunt. The least she could do was call me by my first name.

"I'm sure she's fine, Andrea. She's probably staying with a friend," I told her. See? I wasn't lying to the judge. Jamie *was* staying with a friend. Me.

"Yes, well I hope you're correct. If you see her, will you please ask her to call me? Tell her I just want to make sure she's all right."

"Sure. I'll do that."

"Thank you, Charles," she said, disconnecting.

I put my phone back on the nightstand next to my bed. "I'm supposed to tell you to call your stepmother," I told Jamie, as if she hadn't heard the call.

"Okay. Thanks for taking the message." She resumed grinding on my dick. "I suppose I *should* go home, you know. She sounded worried."

"Yeah, she did."

"You gonna miss me when I'm gone, Charlie?"

"Fucking right I'm gonna miss you. Big time. I haven't had this much fun in a long time. You know, I get a lot of sex because of my job, but that's business sex. It's not the same as what we've been doing – fucking just for the fun of it. And your pussy's a dream, Jamie. So wet, so tight."

"I'm gonna miss you too, Charlie." She rocked back and forth, sliding Junior in and out of one of the greediest cunts he'd ever had the good fortune to visit. I really didn't have to put out much effort at all – just lie there, keep Junior stiff, and hold her by the hips so she didn't fall off. "I'm really gonna miss Junior. I love this big guy."

I chuckled. "He's definitely gonna miss you." I reached up and tweaked her nipple, getting a moan in return.

"Mmm," she said, changing from sliding into more of a *bouncing* motion.

"But me and Junior are both looking forward to catching up on our rest, you know."

"You're tired?"

"Exhausted."

"But you just spent like three days in bed."

"Not particularly restful, for some reason." I grinned at her as she bounced up and down, throwing in a slight twisting motion at the same time. "If I were a battery, it would be time to replace me."

"I see. So, ... before you completely run out of energy, can you like, flip us over and give me one more good, pounding fuck to last me until Tuesday night?"

"A *pounding* fuck, huh? I would be more than happy to do that, young lady," I told her, even though that wasn't entirely true. I wasn't going to be 'more than happy.' While I'd certainly be happy to fuck Jamie one last time, like a going-away present or something, I knew I was going to miss having her conveniently located next to me, right here in my bed, always ready to suck me off or fuck me. Still, it would give me at least a couple of days for the developing friction burns on my dick to heal up. That wasn't something I'd ever had to deal with before but too much fucking comes with a price, evidently.

I rolled us over, managing to keep Junior plugged in as I did so. Jamie wrapped her legs around me, gave me a nasty grin, and said, "Do it, Charlie. Fuck me good."

So I did it. I slammed my dick into that slick, heavenly pussy of hers, over and over. And as I did, I leaned down and whispered in her ear, describing to her what that felt like – just how good her tight little cunt was making me feel.

"Oh, fuck!" she said as I talked to her. She grabbed my ass and tried to pull me into her even harder.

I moaned and closed my eyes as my balls began to stir, warning my dick to get ready. "Fuck, Jamie, your pussy feels *soooo* good. So fucking good!"

"Are you gonna cum?" she said, checking my face for signs I might do just that.

"I'm thinking about it," I told her.

"Mmm. Me, too. And soon."

"Yeah?"

"Uh-huh. Big time. I need one last glorious orgasm to last me until Tuesday. So let me cum first. Okay?"

"Sure. Go ahead. But you better make it quick. Anything I can do to help?"

"Just keep pumping. Oh, maybe a finger up my butt? That might help."

"Only one?"

"One's good. Two's better. But start with one."

I slid my hand under her and pushed my middle finger up her ass, getting, "Unhh," as a comment when it penetrated her. "How's that? Good?"

"One more," she said.

I added my ring finger to the mix.

"Mmm, that's good. Just keep them in place and pound my pussy, please."

Jamie was certainly polite. You have to like a girl who adds *please* when she asks you to fuck her. I smiled to myself as I did just what she'd asked me to do and pounded her pussy with great enthusiasm.

Chapter 22

With Jamie gone, things got back to normal, more or less. I finally managed to drag my lazy ass out of bed and get some work done. I cleaned up my apartment – the place was a mess – stripped my bed and washed the sheets, and spent hours catching up on the editing I'd been neglecting.

Judging by the color – an attractive pink – you'd assume my dick was suffering from a sunburn. Which would have been really weird, I thought, considering the amount of time dicks actually got to loll about, sunning themselves. Of course, in reality, Junior's *sunburn* was caused by his excessive contact with the various private parts of Jamie's anatomy. Whatever, by Monday evening, the pink that had been threatening my dick with friction burns had faded away, I'd caught up on my sleep, and I was back in full, *ready-to-fuck* mode.

"Hey," Joey said when he showed up at the studio Monday night. As usual, he was early.

"Hey," I said back to him.

"How's the cold?"

"Better. All gone. Feeling great."

"Good." He went into the kitchen and grabbed two beers, then came back, handed one to me, and joined me on the couch. "Gimme some of that," he said, nodding at the joint I was smoking.

I took a hit and passed the joint over to him. "So, what did you do during your little vacation?" I said, blowing smoke upward and wondering how long it would take a dark spot to develop on my new ceiling.

"Not much. Went to the dojo and worked out a couple of times – Yoshi said you didn't show up for your classes Saturday morning."

"Yeah, I forgot to call him and tell him I was sick. What else did you do?"

"Spent a lot of time in bed with Megan, of course. And we spent a lot of time in the shower, too. Peeing on each other – just practicing, you know."

I laughed. "You guys are still planning on making a piss video?"

"Yup. I kinda like it. It feels, ... good when she pees on me. Nice and warm. I think she likes it when I pee on her, too." He took a big hit off the joint and held it.

I shook my head and watched him as he held his breath until his face started turning red. When he finally exhaled, hardly any smoke came out. "Hey, don't get *too* stoned," I told him. "Muffin will be here in a half-hour and she'll be expecting you to be able to perform."

"Yeah, Muffin. I really like her. She's sweet. Cute for a fat girl, don'cha think?"

"Muffin's not fat, Joey. She's just, ... kinda meaty. And soft. Really soft."

"She is, isn't she? Nice and soft."

"Yup. And you're right, she's sweet. And cute as fuck."

"Definitely. Sucks a mean dick, too."

I took a drink of my beer. "Yup. That she does."

"Not as good as Jamie, though."

"You think?" I said, casting a glance at him.

"Yeah. Jamie's the best. Nobody sucks cock better than she does. I love it – the way she just attacks your dick with so much enthusiasm, with that gleam in her eyes. If I wasn't working – just fooling around with her for fun, you know – I'll bet she could suck me off in less than five minutes. From scratch. From a limp dick to blowing my load."

You have no idea what an inaccurate description that is, Joey. Less than five minutes? I'm pretty sure she could drain just about any guy's dick in less than one minute if she really wanted to. When it comes to sucking cock, Jamie has mad skills.

That's what I was thinking. What I said was, "Probably. She's good. No doubt about that."

The joint we'd been smoking died and he tossed the roach into the ashtray, lighting another – one he'd actually brought with him. Usually he just showed up and smoked *my* weed. "Yup. I really like her. A lot. She's one of the most fun girls we've ever had."

"Huh. It's weird you'd say that."

"Weird, how?"

"You told her she was crazy. At least a couple of times."

"She *is* crazy. Crazy about dick," he said, laughing.

I laughed, too. Jamie definitely *was* crazy about dick. I knew that for a fact after having spent half a week in bed with her. Anything to do with her and a dick and she was up for it. I mean, how many girls other than her say, "Oh boy, oh boy, oh boy!" when you tell them you're thinking about sticking a giant dick up their ass? Or are willing to lie on their back and hang their head over the end of a bed so you can slide that same giant dick straight down their throat? And not gag, either.

"Listen, I didn't tell you this but you know last Tuesday, when I gave her a ride home?"

"Yeah."

"As soon as we got out of the driveway, she leaned over and pulled my dick out of my shorts. Then she popped it into her mouth and sucked on it for the entire trip."

"You're kidding."

"Nope."

"She sucked you off?"

He shook his head. "I didn't cum. But poor Megan. As soon as I got in the house I woke her up and just destroyed her. Fucked her brains out."

"Huh," was all I could think of to say as I sat there, picturing beautiful Jamie with *my* dick in her mouth.

"Was that a car?" Joey said, interrupting my thoughts about all the fun things Jamie liked to do.

"What?"

"I thought I heard a car door slam. Outside."

"Outside, huh?" I said. "Not inside?"

"Fuck you, Charlie," he said, laughing again just as the door opened and Muffin came prancing in, smiling at us and looking hot as fuck in a too small, side-boob flashing, lime green tank top and a really short white skirt. When we smiled back, she lifted the front of her skirt and flashed us, showing us that – like so many of the girls who show up here – she was absent-minded. She'd forgotten to wear underwear.

I liked that. Liked it when a girl showed up ready to go to work. Of course, I probably felt the same way most guys feel about this subject – hot girls of any age should wear short skirts and ditch the underwear, whether they were on their way to work or just cruising the mall.

Chapter 23

Jamie arrived right on time for her Tuesday evening session. Right on time and eager for the next chapter in her porn adventure to begin. Of course, Jamie was always eager for a little suck and fuck, it seemed, so that wasn't unexpected.

"So, everything okay at home, now?" I asked her. We were sitting on the couch – me, her, and Joey – going through our usual warm-up routine of drinking beer, smoking weed, and me and Joey trying to keep Jamie from playing with our dicks.

"Oh, yeah," she said, casually edging her hand into my lap. "We came to an understanding."

I pushed her hand away, encouraging her to save her *enthusiasm* for later, when we could record it. "What kind of understanding?"

"We made a deal. She's gonna start treating me like an adult and I'm gonna start paying rent."

"Rent?"

"Yeah. Room and board. She said if I'm gonna be an adult and do adult stuff – like what I'm doing here with you guys – then I gotta start paying my own way."

I nodded and took a drink of my beer, wondering why the joint we were smoking never seemed to make it down to my end of the couch. "That seems fair, I guess. Can you do that until your Fukknumzie money starts coming in – pay rent? You don't have a job or anything."

She giggled. "I don't need a job. My dad's rich. He gives me a huge allowance. Way more than my friends get."

"Yeah? How much does he give you?" Joey said, joining our conversation.

"Three hundred a week."

He gave her a disbelieving look. "You're kidding, right?"

"Nope. Ever since I got my driver's license. I was only getting two hundred before that, but when I turned 16 and got my license, he bought me a car and said I was probably gonna need more money. You know, for insurance and gas and stuff. So he gave me a raise."

"Fuck! I wish I'd had rich parents."

"Me, too," I said. Yup. Growing up with rich parents would have been nice.

"Besides, Andrea's only gonna charge me a hundred a month. So rent's not gonna be a problem," Jamie said.

"Guess not." I glanced at my wall clock. "We should get going pretty soon."

"Oh boy, oh boy. What are we gonna do tonight, anyway?"

"I'm not sure," I told her. "I thought I'd leave it up to you, since you kinda threw our regular schedule out of whack by adding that pussy-eating video."

"Yeah, but that was fun, wasn't it?"

"Uh-huh. It was."

"You know, back when you told me about how you turned five videos into 15, you said one of the five was a blowjob video. Right?"

"Yup."

"So, we haven't done that yet. Let's do it tonight. I'm definitely in the mood to suck some dick."

Joey laughed and said, "You're *always* in the mood to suck dick, aren't you, Jamie?"

"Pretty much," she said, grinning at him and not looking at all embarrassed, the way some girls do when you start discussing their cocksucking talent.

"Yeah, we can do that tonight," I said. "That's what you wanna do? A straight blowjob video?"

"Well, since there are two of you, we can throw in some other stuff, too, I guess. Some 69, for sure. Maybe some fucking. As long as I keep a dick in my mouth most of the time, we can call it a blowjob video, can't we?"

"Absolutely," I said. I leaned forward and glanced over at Joey, sitting there with a smirk on his face. Caused, no doubt, by Jamie's *enthusiasm*. "You almost ready?"

He nodded, tipping his beer up and draining the bottle. "I *am* ready," he said, adding a burp for emphasis.

I looked at Jamie and she said, "Oh boy, oh boy." So she was ready, too.

"Let's go, then," I said.

* * *

Over the course of the next few hours, Jamie did what she had to do in order to call this a blowjob video – she kept either mine or Joey's dick in her mouth pretty much at all times, regardless of what was happening with the rest of her body. After we took turns sixty-nining with her – both with her on the bottom and on top – Joey spent some time slurping her cute little pussy while she occupied herself by snacking on Junior. Then Joey and I switched places and she attempted to swallow his dick while I ate her out. She even sucked both our dicks at the same time while Joey finger-fucked her cunt and I finger-fucked her ass. Getting into realistic-looking positions for that scene was actually a little awkward. I wasn't sure I'd be able to use any of that footage in her video, but it was fun doing it.

Until right at the end, when we splashed an evening's worth of held-back cum onto a kneeling Jamie's face and down her throat, no orgasms had been involved in the evening's activities – at least, not for Joey and me. Jamie got off twice – both times while she was getting her pussy munched. That seemed to be one of her favorite pursuits. That and sucking dick, of course – Jamie *loved* having a dick in her mouth.

By the time we were all sitting on the couch, wrapping up our session in the same way we always did – with beer and weed – the three of us were feeling pretty satisfied. At least, I assumed the two people sitting next to me were satisfied. I knew *I* was. Satisfied with both our evening session and the fact that Junior had finally been able to dump his load. Right onto Jamie.

"So, we've got a couple more weeks, huh?" she said, taking a sip of her beer.

"Uh-huh."

"What are we gonna do next week?"

"Cowgirl and reverse cowgirl," I told her.

"Riding, huh?"

"Yup. Riding."

"I really like riding, you know. I like being on top."

"I know you do, sweetie." I took a hit off the joint as Jamie passed it to me, then handed it back to her.

"And then the final session. Buttfucking. Right?"

"Yup. That's what you said you wanted for your fifth video."

"I do. I'm looking forward to sitting on that big dick of yours," she said.

Joey smirked and shook his head in disbelief, getting an elbow in the ribs and a "Yours, too, Joey," from Jamie.

"Have you no shame, Jamie?" he said.

"Not when it comes to dicks and my butt, evidently," she said, laughing.

"Hey, you hear that?"

"What?" she said.

"I thought I heard a car."

"Outside?" I said.

"Yeah, outside." Joey grinned at our private joke.

"Oh, that's probably for me," Jamie said, hopping off the couch, draining the rest of her beer, and putting the empty bottle on the coffee table. "Gotta go. See you guys next week. Don't forget to bring your saddles. Or am I gonna have to ride bareback?"

"No saddles. Bareback," I told her.

"You don't need a ride home tonight?" Joey said, looking slightly disappointed.

"Nope. I've got a ride. Someone's picking me up."

"Yeah? Who?"

"Someone." She grinned at him as she backed up across the living room.

"Someone?"

"Yeah, just, ... someone," she said, trying to make her voice sound mysterious. Then she toodle-oohed us with her fingers and disappeared out the door. The sounds of a car door slamming and then a car leaving the driveway filtered into the room.

"Someone's picking her up?" Joey said.

"Look like it."

"I wonder who."

"No idea."

"Hmm," he said, wiggling his eyebrows and doing his own impression of a mysterious-sounding voice. "And just like that, the plot thickens."

"You're a fucking idiot, you know that, Joey? She probably just called an Uber when she was in the bathroom," I said, and he laughed. But I couldn't help wondering if maybe he was right, if maybe the arrival of Jamie's *mysterious* ride home signaled some change in the dynamics of our relationship and maybe the plot *was* going to get thicker. It was odd that she wouldn't tell us who was picking her up.

Chapter 24

"It's Buttfuck Tuesday," Jamie announced as she bounced through the front door, looking happy as a Pismo Beach clam. I don't know why people – including me, evidently – use that expression, actually. Are clams ever really, *truly* happy? Any type of clams?

"I am *soooo* hungry," Jamie continued. "I haven't had anything to eat since breakfast yesterday."

"You can eat my dick if you want," Joey said.

She gave him a serious look and licked her lips, as if she was considering his offer. "Can I cook it first?" she said.

"Actually, it tastes better when you eat it raw."

She laughed and headed into the kitchen, coming back with a beer and flopping down onto the couch, between Joey and me.

"How'd you get here tonight?" Joey asked her.

"Uber."

"Really? You're sure?"

"Of course I'm sure." She grinned, mostly to herself, as if she knew something we didn't know. Which she did, of course. She knew who had picked her up after her last two sessions and we didn't, because she wouldn't tell us. And she was driving us – especially Joey – nuts, teasing us by withholding the information.

We'd spent the previous Tuesday – our *ride 'em, cowgirl* session – trying to get her to tell us the identity of the mysterious stranger who'd provided her with a ride home the week before, when we'd been doing all that blowjob stuff. But she wouldn't do it. No matter what we offered her as an inducement to confess who it was, she wouldn't say. We'd even tried to trick her into telling us, but the only answer we'd been able to get out of her was the vague, "Someone," delivered with a gloating, shit-eating grin.

And then, at the end of the evening, the same thing had happened. A ride home for her miraculously appeared at midnight, seemingly without her doing anything to make that happen. And she'd refused to tell us who the driver was, conjuring up her usual answer – *someone* – before vanishing into the night.

Joey had wanted to go outside and see who was driving the car but I talked him out of it. I knew he was curious because he was slightly upset – whoever it was, they were depriving him of the chance to drive home with Jamie's warm, wet mouth *smooching* his dick. But it really wasn't any of our business, when you got right down to it. Besides, Jamie not wanting us to know the identity of her secret, midnight driver was fine with me. I'd already convinced myself it was an Uber driver and she'd just scheduled a midnight pick-up.

"Who's that?" Jamie looked at me as the sound of a car pulling into the driveway drifted into the living room. "You expecting someone?"

I shrugged. "Dunno."

"Oh, yeah," Joey said. "That's probably Megan. She said she might drop by to offer encouragement to you, Jamie."

"Encouragement? Why would she do that? We don't even know each other."

"Yeah, but because she's the Buttfuck Queen of the West, she knows that taking giant dicks up your butt isn't the easiest thing for a rookie to get used to. I guess she figured you could use a friendly face, rooting you on."

"Megan? Your girlfriend, Megan? She's Bonnie the Buttfuck Queen?"

"Yeah, she is."

"How come you never mentioned that before?"

He took a pull off his beer. "Never came up, I guess."

Joey stood as the door opened and Megan came in, looking hot as fuck in short-shorts and a tank top, her thick, dark hair tied back in a ponytail. She looked around, taking in the newly remodeled living room with an *impressed* look on her face. Although she'd seen the place when I'd first taken possession of it, this was the first time she'd been here since then. "Wow, it's really nice, you guys. You did a great job of fixing it up." When she noticed Jamie, sitting on the couch next to me, she walked over to us. "So you're Jamie, huh?" she said as she motioned for Joey to go into the kitchen and fetch her a beer.

"Yeah, I am," Jamie said, looking slightly intimidated by Megan's presence as they shook hands. "And you're Bonnie, the Buttfuck Queen of the West. I am soooo happy to meet you. I've got all five of your long-form videos on my laptop."

"Call me Megan, or better yet, Meg. That's my real name," Megan said, smiling and sitting down next to her. "And fuck, Joey told me you were good looking but you're beautiful. Absolutely gorgeous. I see now why he's been so eager to go to work on Tuesdays." She cast a suspicious glance at her boyfriend just as he arrived back at the couch with a handful of beers but he just grinned at her.

Jamie blushed, not something that was a normal part of her arsenal, and offered a mumbled, "Thank you."

Joey handed out beers and took a seat next to Megan. "Don't fib, sweetie. I told you she was one of the best-looking girls I'd ever seen. And definitely one of the sweetest looking, too."

"Thank you, Joey." Jamie's blush deepened, heading toward red.

Megan nodded, agreeing with her boyfriend. "She is. *Super* sweet looking. And so young looking, too. You *are* 18, aren't you, Jamie?"

Jamie nodded, her face now a bright red. "Uh-huh. I am."

"The pervs are gonna make you rich in no time at all," Megan told her, patting her on the leg.

"The pervs?"

"Yeah. The guys who like *really* young girls. They're gonna love you 'cause you look so young and innocent."

"That's a good thing, right?"

"Oh, yeah. When it comes to making money on Fukknumzie, that's a *very* good thing."

"Well, that's what I wanna do, you know," Jamie said. "Make a lot of money."

Megan laughed. "That's definitely gonna happen. And so quick – once the money starts coming in, you're gonna be rolling in it."

"I can live with that, I guess," Jamie said, laughing along with her as she began to relax.

"So listen, do you do girls, too?"

"Do what? Girls?"

"Yeah. You know. Lesbian stuff. Eating pussy, scissoring. Girl stuff – no dicks needed."

"Oh. Well, I haven't. But I'd be willing to, I guess. Why? Are you a lesbian?"

"Nope. I like dicks. But adding in a little girl-girl action helps you sell more downloads. Lots of guys get off on that stuff."

"Oh, okay."

"If you want to, maybe we could add some of that into your session tonight."

"With you, you mean?"

"I'm the only other girl here besides you, Jamie." Megan chuckled.

Jamie grinned at her. "Yeah, that's true, isn't it?" She looked at me. "Can we do something like that, Charlie? Put Megan in my video, I mean."

"I don't know. You wanna get paid for your performance, Meg?"

"No need. Just a credit is fine."

"Then sure. We can list her as a special guest star. And I'll add in some links to her videos."

"Oh boy!" Jamie said. "Me and Bonnie the Buttfuck Queen of the West in the same video. Oh boy, oh boy, oh boy!"

Oh boy, indeed. Tonight's session looked to be something special. Something *really* special!

Chapter 25

"I've been thinking," I said as the four of us trekked down the hall to the studio.

"Oh, oh," Jamie said. "I hope this isn't about my ear."

Megan glanced at her. "What's this about your ear?"

"Uh, in my early enthusiasm, I might have told Charlie he could fuck me in the ear if he wanted to."

"What!! In your *ear*? And ... did he? Did he try to do that?"

I laughed. "I didn't fuck her ear, Megan. We don't do earjobs here at Jumbo Johnson Productions."

"Well, I would hope the fuck not! A girl would have to have an awfully big ear. Although, I think you did *cum* in my ear, once."

"That was an accident," I said. "I was aiming for your mouth."

Jamie leaned over and whispered at Meg, loud enough for all of us to hear, "You fucked Charlie before? Really?"

"Oh, yeah. Like a thousand times. I love that big dick of his. Don't I, Joey?" She grinned at her boyfriend.

He grinned back at her. "Fuck you, Meg."

"You'll get your chance," she said, laughing.

"Promises, promises."

"Joey and I have an arrangement," Megan explained to Jamie. "He fucks who he wants and I fuck who I want. And there's just something about Charlie's dick, you know. I really like it. It's so, ... *thick!* It really fills you up."

Jamie giggled. "I know. Thick is *soooo* good. I love Charlie's dick."

"Hey," Joey said. "Could you girls talk about something else. You're gonna give me an inferiority complex."

Megan ignored him, continuing her conversation with Jamie. "Did he fuck you in the ass yet?"

"Not yet."

"Ooh, you're in for a treat. But start with Joey. Let him warm you up – his little fuck stick is – "

"Hey! My fuck stick is *not* little!"

"Yeah, that's true, I guess. But it's not as thick as Charlie's."

Jamie giggled some more. "I don't think any other guy has a dick as thick as Charlie's. Or as delicious."

"You're right about that," Megan said, nodding.

Joey put his head in his hands. "Fuck! Stop! You guys are ruining me. I probably won't even be able to get a hard-on."

"Bet you will," Megan said, making Jamie laugh.

"Okay, okay." I clapped my hands. "Time to go to work."

"Oh boy!" Jamie said. "As far as work goes, this is the best job *ever*!"

I definitely agreed with that sentiment. "So, as I started to say, earlier, I have an idea but it's up to you guys. I was thinking we could feature you both tonight, more or less equally, and then I could edit the footage into two videos – one emphasizing Jamie and one emphasizing Meg. So you'd each get a video. Then I could cross link them, you know. That way, guys who like to see girls getting their assholes reamed by big dicks will be aware of both of you and maybe they'll buy videos from you both. Whaddaya think? Would that be okay?"

Jamie and Meg looked at each other and then they both agreed.

"Great. So let's get the two of you out of your clothes and up onto the bed and we'll start with some girl-girl action."

Joey and I watched as the girls stripped off their clothes. They'd learned long ago not to wear panties or bras to their sessions – those items left lines and indentations on the skin that took forever to disappear – so that only took about 10 seconds. The two of them stood there, naked, looking at us with expectant expressions.

"Like what you see?" Meg said.

Joey nodded and I said, "Yup. Like it a lot. So, ... up on the bed. Start with a little making out, then one of you – doesn't matter which one – slide down and eat some pussy. After a while, switch places, so we get lots of good footage of each of you munching cunt. Then eventually, I want you to end up sixty-nining each other. Again, doesn't matter who's on top, who's on the bottom."

"How will we know when to switch positions," Jamie said.

"I'll tell you. Anyway, after we get a lot of lezzie stuff, Joey will join you while you're in 69 position and he'll fuck you both – one of you doggy style and the other one in the mouth. Back and forth, you know."

"Doggy style in the ass or the pussy?"

"Pussy. And I'm gonna join in on that cunt to mouth stuff, too. Down at the other end. I'm gonna need a lot of warm-up footage, you know, to have enough for two separate videos. So depending on how long that all takes, maybe there'll be time for some one on one pussy eating, cocksucking, things like that – the regular stuff we do. We'll see. Whatever, after all that, we'll get into some buttfucking." I paused to let everyone consider what I'd just said. "So, are we all good with that plan?"

"Sounds good to me," Megan said and Jamie added, "Oh, boy!" The girls climbed up onto the bed and lay there, waiting side by side, as Joey and I picked up camcorders and got into position to film the scene.

"Okay then, start making out," I said.

Both girls continued lying there, not doing anything, for about five seconds. I was just about to tell them to get going when Megan rolled over, putting herself in an almost-on-top position. She palmed Jamie's left breast and pinched her nipple, rolling it between her thumb and forefinger, then leaned down and kissed her.

Jamie responded by wrapping her arms around Megan and kissing her back. Enthusiastically. Soft moaning sounds arose from the bed, although it was impossible to tell which of the two girls was responsible – maybe it was both of them. Jamie's hand slid down Meg's back and grabbed a handful of ass.

Joey and I wandered around the bed, filming them from various angles. And yeah, I know – no film is required for digital videography, so we weren't really *filming* anything. But using the words *videoing* and *recording* just sounded weird, while *filming* sounded natural.

When I felt we had enough footage of them making out, I told them, "Okay, time to eat some pussy."

Meg took the initiative, licking her way down Jamie's neck and chest, stopping at her breasts to suck each nipple until they looked like they'd achieved hard-on status, then continuing downward. For her part, Jamie giggled and tossed in, "That tickles! But in a *good* way." I wasn't sure whether or not I'd be able to use that in the final video. Jamie was turning out to be quite the giggler. I briefly wondered if she was extra nervous about doing this girl-girl stuff, then decided that, as long as she was willing to go through with it, I didn't really give a fuck if she was nervous or not. I was pretty sure I could make her look good in the final edit.

Chapter 26

Megan ate pussy the same way she sucked dick – with great enthusiasm. She licked. She slurped. She pushed Jamie's legs wide open and tongue-fucked her while she diddled her clit – Jamie's clit, not her own – with her thumb.

Jamie moaned. And groaned. And writhed. She slapped the bed with both hands as Meg used her fingers to spread that juicy cunt apart and pushed her tongue in and out of that tight, slippery hole. If Jamie was faking her reactions, she was doing an excellent job, but I didn't think she was pretending. After all, if a girl closed her eyes, it's likely a female tongue slurping her pussy would feel just as good as when a male tongue did it. Maybe even better, since presumably a girl would know exactly what it feels like down there and know what to do to get the best results. Or maybe it made no difference at all – a tongue was a tongue and a cunt was a cunt, and when they bumped into each other, they had fun. Anyway, how the fuck would I know what it felt like? I was a guy.

I forced myself to look away from Jamie's pussy and glanced up at her face. Yup. Her eyes were closed.

"Fuck, this is good stuff," Joey said, moving in for an extreme closeup.

I nodded. Joey was right, this was going to make a great-looking video. But it was time for the girls to swap places – time for Jamie to slurp Megan's cunt for a while. I was just about to tell them to switch when Jamie made a move that caused me to change my mind.

She had an orgasm. A wild, screaming, bouncing-around-the-bed, leg-shaking orgasm of the kind no girl could fake, no matter how skillful an actress she was. There was no doubt about it – Jamie was definitely *not* faking.

A long and extremely loud moan was the first clue that something was about to happen. She grasped Megan and pulled her face tightly against her pussy, then wrapped her legs around her head and began to, ... *vibrate*, her entire body just shaking. "Ohhhhhhhh, fuuuuuuuck!!" she screamed as she began to porpoise around the bed like one of those marine mammals slicing through water. Megan grabbed her by the hips and held on for the ride, even though she really didn't have much choice but to go along, what with Jamie's legs being locked around her head in what looked like a wrestling move.

"Oh boy, so good, so good," Jamie said when she finally stopped bouncing. She pulled Meg up and kissed her. "That was *soooo* fucking good! I think I love you, Megan."

Megan laughed. Joey laughed, then let his face settle into a huge, *that's-my-girl* grin, as if to say, "Can my girl eat pussy or *what*!" And I laughed, too, saying, "I think Jamie just loves orgasms, no matter how she gets them."

"I do, I do," she said. "And oh boy, that was a good one. *Really* good!"

"You need a little break?" I asked her.

"Gimme two minutes. Just lemme catch my breath, okay? I feel weak." She lay there, a happy look on her face, her tits rising and falling as she panted, her right hand between her legs, gently massaging her cunt as it leaked moisture onto the bed. Jamie was the possessor of an extremely *juicy* pussy.

My dick – Junior – was so hard it hurt. I was tempted to climb on top of her and fuck that pleased, silly look right off her face. But I didn't, of course. I acted like the professional I was supposed to be.

"Sure. Take your time," I said, knowing I'd get to bury my stiffy in her, later on – in her mouth, in her cunt, and tonight, for the first time, in her ass. And maybe, just for the fun of it, I'd find out what it felt like to cum in her ear, too. That would teach her not make promises she didn't intend to keep.

Once Jamie had rested up and regained her strength, the girls got back to work. It was Jamie's turn to munch cunt. Not surprisingly, she attacked Meg's pussy with her usual, oh-boy-oh-boy enthusiasm, slurping that slit from bottom to top, always stopping for some leisurely tonguing of clitoris before returning to the bottom to begin the trip again.

Megan arched her back and moaned. She pinched her own nipples and groaned. And then, as Joey passed by her, relocating to a new position, she reached out and grabbed his dick. "C'mere, you," she said, pulling it close to her. Joey, like most guys a slave to his dick, followed along, ending up next to her, kneeling on the bed.

Tugging Little Joey – Megan's pet name for Joey's dick – down to her mouth, she buzzed his dickhead, vibrating her lips against the tip and making him jump. She laughed, saying, "You like that, do you?"

"Fuck, Meg. You know I do. I love it when you do that."

"Call her Bonnie," I reminded him.

"Fuck yeah I do, Bonnie," he said. "I love it."

"I love it, too," she said, sucking Little Joey into her mouth and deep down her throat.

Joey moaned and leaned back, watching her as she gobbled his dick. He seemed to have forgotten he was supposed to be recording all this so I motioned for him to aim his camcorder down at her and record what Meg was doing from his point of view, the way *he* was seeing it. Guys liked to watch POV scenes, I knew – it let them pretend it was them fucking the girl's mouth or pussy while they jerked off.

After a minute or so of sliding his dick in and out of Megan's mouth, he turned to me. "Fuck, this feels so good. Can I cum, Charlie? I mean, ... Jumbo."

"The answer is no but ask me again, anyway. And say it right."

"Fuck, this feels so good. Can I cum, Jumbo?"

"No. Save it for later," I told him, getting a disappointed look in return.

Down below, between Meg's legs, Jamie had stayed busy throughout this unplanned-for deviation from our script. As I aimed my camcorder back at her – I'd been filming Joey face-fucking Meg so we'd have the scene from two different viewpoints – she was finger-fucking Megan's cunt with two fingers while at same time letting her tongue dance back and forth across her swollen clit. Once again I marveled at how quickly a young, inexperienced girl like Jamie could adapt so quickly to the skills necessary to become a successful porn actress. The girl was a natural.

Chapter 27

I moved my big camera. Actually, it wasn't that big but it was mounted on a tripod and that gave it more status than the handheld camcorders we used. So I always called it my *big* camera. Anyway, I repositioned it, moving it more to the side of the bed and closer to the action.

"Fluff me up a little bit more, will ya?" Joey said, tapping his dick on his girlfriend's forehead.

The girls had segued from what they'd been doing – taking turns eating each other's pussy – into their current placement. Jamie lay in reverse position on top of Megan, straddling her with her cunt firmly planted on Meg's mouth. On the bottom, her arms wrapped around Jamie's butt, Meg's mouth returned the favor, munching Jamie's pussy. Some people refer to this as *the 69 position*, I've heard.

Temporarily abandoning Jamie's glistening cunt, wet with both saliva and leaking pussy juice, Meg leaned her head back and opened her mouth.

"Do you really need her to do that?" I asked Joey as he slid his dick into her waiting mouth. "You've already got a hard-on."

"True. But I need this for, like, ... inspiration, you know."

I chuckled. "Yeah, right. Inspiration. Well, as soon as you're *inspired*, let's move on. Okay?"

"Sure."

"You're gonna be fucking her mouth half the time, anyway, in this scene."

"Yeah." He grinned. "And the other half of the time I'll be slipping it into Jamie's sweet, juicy little pussy. I can hardly wait. Jamie's pussy is so smooth and tight and clingy, it's like fucking a pussy from heaven. You know?"

Although I definitely agreed with Joey's assessment of Jamie's pussy – even though he'd forgotten to include the word *tasty* in his description – I started to remind him that Jamie's porn name was Stella.

But I was interrupted when he suddenly jumped backward and said, "Ouch!" in a loud voice. He glared at his girlfriend. "What the *fuck*, Megan! What are you doing?"

Her head still leaning back, Meg said, "Sorry," attempting an upside-down innocent look. "It was an accident."

"The fuck it was!"

"What happened?" I said.

"She *bit* me!"

I couldn't help it – I laughed, even though I knew from experience that getting a dick bite was *not* a lot of fun. Especially if it was your *dickhead* that suffered the bite. "Teach you to praise another girl's pussy when your dick's in her mouth," I told him. "You should know better."

Jamie laughed, too, judging by the way her midsection was bouncing up and down. But her mouth never lost contact with Meg's pussy and no sound escaped as her laugh disappeared up that dark, wet tunnel between Megan's legs.

Megan continued trying to look innocent but I could tell she was having a hard time not joining in the laughter. "Really sorry, you know," she said in a completely insincere voice.

"Fuck! I don't think I can continue," Joey said, rubbing his dick, which was no longer hard. "Do I have worker's comp, Charlie? This is a workplace injury."

I laughed some more. "No, you don't. But I'll drive you to the emergency room if you want."

"Fuck you guys." He moved down to where Jamie was still busily slurping Meg's pussy. "Hey, sweetie, how about fluffing up your favorite dick for me?" he asked her.

She looked up at him, saying, "Sorry, Joey. I like your dick but it's not my favorite. That dick belongs to Jumbo."

"Whatever. Can you just give it a few sucks, help me get it hard again?"

"Hmm, I don't know. I'd like to help you out but what will Megan say?"

"She won't mind."

From down at the other end of the bed, a threatening female voice said, "Are you *sure*, Joey?" making the room fill with laughter. None of that laughter came from Joey, however.

"All right, all right. Let's stop fooling around and get back to work," I said. "We've still got a lot to get done."

"I'm ready," Joey said.

"Your dick's okay? Able to perform its duties?"

He looked down. "Yeah. Little Joey's fine, I guess."

"Good. Then we might as well go ahead and get started with some cunt to mouth fucking. I'll let you have Jamie's mouth and Meg's pussy and I'll take the other end. That way you won't be worried that Meg might *accidentally* bite your dick again. Okay?"

He nodded. "You're the boss."

"Yeah, I am, ain't I?" I said, grinning at him.

"Yup."

I turned to Jamie, who'd stopped licking Megan's pussy and was looking up at me. "You've got the top position and that's a little more complicated than what Meg has to do," I told her. "First of all, you've got to keep your head out of the way. You can't eat her pussy while Joey's fucking it, okay? There's not enough room and even if you could get your head in there at the same time, you'd be blocking the camera's view."

"Okay."

I picked up a towel, leaned forward, and wiped off saliva and pussy juice from where it was dripping off her chin, onto the bed, then handed her the towel so she could wipe the rest of her face. "So you can play with his balls or do something with your hands while he's doing that. And I want you to count to five, slowly – not out loud, of course, just in your head – while Joey's fucking her, then reach down and pull his dick out of her cunt and pop it into your mouth and let him face-fuck you for another five-count. Then pull it out and plug it back into Megan. Back and forth in five-second intervals. Got it?"

"Got it."

"You're sure?"

"Jeez, I'm not a moron, you know. Just because I'm a slut doesn't mean I'm stupid. I like dick – so sue me."

"You're not a slut, sweetie," I told her.

"Oh, come on, Charlie. I mean, Jumbo. I know what guys call girls like me, girls who like sex just as much as they do. They're *studs* and we're *sluts*!"

"Nope. Not to me. As far as I'm concerned you're not a slut, you're a cute little *fuckbunny*."

She considered the term, looking pensive. "I'm a fuckbunny?"

"Yup. Not a slut. A fuckbunny."

"I like that," she said, smiling up at me. "I like it a *lot*!"

Chapter 28

Now that Jamie, one of my all-time favorite *fuckbunnies*, had her directions for the scene, we got started. Joey knew what to do, of course – he'd done this before. Many times. And Jamie ... well, if you didn't know how young she was, how inexperienced she had to be, you'd swear she'd done this before, too. Also many times. As I've said – she was a natural when it came to this sucky-fucky stuff.

The girls returned to their cunt-munching activities and Joey walked into the scene, massaging his already-firm dick with his hand. He stopped down at Jamie's end and watched for a few seconds as she ate Meg's pussy. I filmed his entrance with my camcorder – the big camera was too close to the action to pick him up until he was part of it and I didn't want it to look like he'd just suddenly appeared, as if by magic.

"Hi, Stella," he said, remembering to call Jamie by her porn name.

She looked up at him, her face all wet and ... drippy. "Hey, Joey, you made it," she said.

"Uh-huh. Looks like you started without me, though."

"Yeah, we got hungry so we decided to have a little lunch." She leaned over and gave Meg's slit a long, slurpy lick, then looked back up at him, batted her eyelashes, and smiled, dribbling drool down onto Meg's pussy as she did so.

Joey chuckled and he climbed up onto the bed, kneeling between Megan's legs, his dick inches away from Jamie's mouth. Then he offered it to her. Which, of course, she accepted, sucking Little Joey into her mouth as if that was the most natural reaction in the world to finding a naked guy waving his dick around in front of you while you were trying to eat your girlfriend's pussy. After all, we were making a porn video and that's the way things work in the wonderful world of pornography.

But wow. I was so impressed. I hadn't told Jamie to say any of that. In fact, I hadn't told her to say *anything*. She'd improvised the scene and made it sound like a natural conversation two people might have if they encountered each other while one of them was eating pussy and the other one just happened to be wandering around, naked, playing with his dick. She'd even made it slightly humorous by referring to what she and Megan were doing as *having a little lunch*. Fuck, Jamie wasn't just a natural at the sucky-fucky stuff, she could *act*, too.

However, as Joey slid his dick back and forth between Jamie's plump, glistening lips, the time for her to turn Little Joey over to Megan's pussy, patiently waiting below for its turn, approached, arrived, and passed. But Jamie kept slurping. She'd apparently forgotten my instructions about counting to five.

"Jamie?" I said.

She slipped Little Joey out of her mouth and let him rest on her chin as she glanced up at me, looking slightly annoyed, as if I'd interrupted her fun. "What?"

"Did you forget? You're supposed to share Joey's dick with Megan. You're supposed to count to five and then plug it into her."

"I am counting."

"You are?" That was weird. I knew I'd told her to count slowly but, c'mon, Joey's dick had been in her mouth for at least 30 seconds when I'd interrupted them. How slow could she count?

"Yeah, but I'm only up to three and a half," she said.

"Three and a half? How are you counting, anyway?"

"By eighths," she said, adding a giggle.

"What!"

"You know. One eighth, two eighths, three eighths, like that. And when you get to one, then it's one and one eighth, one and two eighths, one and –"

"Fuck, Jamie! Stop screwing around and do what you're supposed to or we're gonna be here all night," I said, trying to sound angry. But she fluttered her eyelashes at me, looking all cute and innocent, and I couldn't do it. I smiled. "Just stop it. Count like normal people count. In whole numbers – 1, 2, 3, 4, 5. Like that. No eighths."

She grinned and repeated the numbers back to me. "Okay. I think I got it."

"Good. Get back to work. Let's start over from where Joey comes in."

Joey wiped his cock, balls, and pubic hair dry with a towel, carefully checking for lint. He picked off a couple of pieces, fluffed up his pubes with his fingers, then took his place near the door. And we began the scene again.

I filmed the action from the side, making sure to stay out of the big camera's vision. After I had three or four minutes of him fucking Megan's pussy and Jamie's mouth back and forth, I picked up another camcorder – there were seemingly a half dozen of them sitting in chairs around the room – and handed it to Joey, telling him, "POV, aim it straight down. And keep it up high where the big camera won't see it."

The big camera was aimed so as to only film Joey and me from the chest down. That's the way we normally filmed things. We tried to keep our faces out of the shots and focus on the stars of the show – the girls, their pussies, and our dicks. Of course, sometimes our faces did show up and I couldn't edit them out. Like when we were eating pussy, for example. It's really hard to film a guy munching cunt without showing his face.

"Okay, I'm gonna join the scene now," I told the group. "Joey, put your camcorder down behind the girls so the big camera won't see it. I wanna get a couple of minutes of you and me fucking both of them at the same time and I'm gonna move it back so we can get everything in the shot."

"Here," he said, handing the camcorder to me. "Just put it on that chair, there, instead."

I did as he asked, then pulled the big camera away from the bed and adjusted the aim. When everything was all set up, in position, I walked into the scene, telling Megan in a soft voice I'd have to edit out, later, "Try not to bite me, Meg," and getting giggles from both ends of the pile of female flesh in front of me.

Chapter 29

I needed fluffing. Junior wasn't exactly *limp*, ... but he wasn't exactly stiff, either. Fortunately, I had just what I needed to firm him up, right in front of me – Jamie's wet, glistening pussy and beneath that, Megan's wet, glistening mouth. Both of them stared at Junior in anticipation. "Suck him up for me, Meg," I told her, rubbing my dickhead on her forehead and along the side of her nose. "Make him hard."

"Mmm, I can do that," she said. She wrapped her fingers around the base of my dick but before she could grab a taste of it she began sliding back and forth, toward me and away from me. So she paused, waiting, and explained her to-and-fro movements. "Joey's in my cunt, now. He's really pounding me – revenge for biting his dick, I guess."

"You like that?"

"Biting dicks?"

I shook my head. "Getting pounded."

"Yeah, sometimes. But not now – not when it's like I'm getting spit-roasted."

"Hey, Joey," I said.

He looked up at me. "Yeah?"

"Ease up a little. Not so hard."

"Where's the fun in that?" he said, grinning.

"It's not a request. Just do it. No pounding – fuck her nice and easy."

"Oh. Okay, sorry. Next time, then. It's Jamie's turn now."

The two-girl pile stopped sliding back and forth as Joey's dick abandoned his girlfriend's pussy and vanished into Jamie's mouth. And after a short pause, my dick – or most of it, anyway – also disappeared. Into Meg's mouth. And then I had what, in retrospect, turned out to be a really bad idea. To remind Jamie of what was about to happen down here at her other end, and without giving her a warning, I plunged my thumb into her pussy. I mean, c'mon. It was right there in front of me, all wet and juicy looking, winking at me – the infamous *vertical* wink – practically begging me to do something. I couldn't resist.

I probably should have warned her, though. Let her know what I was about to do. After all, I not only have a huge dick, my thumbs are oversize, too. Probably bigger than some guys' dicks.

Yup, I definitely should have told her I was about to poke her pussy because, judging by what happened next, it caught her completely by surprise. She jumped. Pretty fucking high, actually. And she said something, too, although I couldn't understand what it was.

Joey also had something to say. I believe it was, "Fuck! Fuuu-uck! Fucking A! Dammit all to fucking hell, Jamie!" Yeah, something like that – that's what he said. And as he said it, he bounced off the bed, danced away from Jamie's mouth, and out of the scene.

Everything stopped. Megan popped my dick out of her mouth, into her hand, and looked up at me. "What happened?" she said.

"Uh, ... well, I'm not exactly sure. But if I had to hazard a guess, ... and judging by the way Joey's bopping around while he's examining his dick, I'd say it looks like Jamie bit him. Bit his dick."

"What?" She started to laugh. "Twice in one night?"

"Yeah. You know when Jamie just jumped? You felt that, right?"

"Uh-huh."

"Well, that was because I surprised her. I stuck my thumb up her cunt. And Joey's dick was in her mouth at the time and well, you know what happened."

"I know I do," she said, a huge grin on her face. "But tell me, anyway."

I shrugged. "More bite marks for Little Joey."

"Poor Little Joey," she said. "Another sad victim of Bitten Dick Syndrome." And then she busted out laughing.

I know most people don't realize it, but *Bitten Dick Syndrome* is a real hazard in the porn industry. What happened to Joey wasn't even all that unusual in a business where so many working hours are spent with dicks in mouths. I've had it happen to me. It probably occurs among amateurs, as well, would be my guess. Just not as often.

"Jamie?" I said.

She looked back at me. "Yeah?"

"No biting."

"It was an accident. You surprised me – for just a second, I thought you had *two* dicks."

"Okay, I'll try to warn you when something like that is about to happen. But at the same time, remember what we're doing here – filming porn – so you shouldn't be *too* surprised when a thumb or a dick suddenly appears in your cunt as if by magic. And if that happens while you've got a dick in your mouth, don't bite it."

"Anyway, it was hardly a bite, more like just a little *nibble*."

"Whatever. Just try not to bite anyone."

"Okay." She giggled and turned back to the front, apparently ready to get back to work.

"You bleeding, Joey?" I asked him.

He was bent over, carefully examining his dick, which had gone soft. His stiffy had turned into a limpy. "No," he said.

"Bruising?"

"It looks all right. Might be some tomorrow. That hurt like a motherfucker, though. She got me right on my dickhead!"

"Too bad. But we've got a lot to do. Let's get back to work."

"Yeah, well I kinda lost my mojo. My hard-on's gone."

"Then let Jamie fluff it back up for you."

He eyed Jamie with suspicion.

"Or come over here and let Meg do it, I don't care," I added.

"I'm not sure I trust either one of them to fluff Little Joey back into working shape."

"Well, *I'm* not gonna do it for you so pick one of the girls, stick your dick in her mouth, and let her suck you hard. C'mon. Let's go."

He climbed back up onto the bed and glared at Jamie. "Can I trust you not to bite me again?" he said.

"Of course you can, Joey. You know that was an accident. You can trust me – it won't happen again."

I couldn't see Jamie's face but from the sound of her voice, I could tell she was almost laughing as she said those words to Joey.

"It better not," he said, offering her his dick. "I don't think Little Joey could handle a third biting incident on the same night."

A brief period of giggling arose from down at Jamie's end, then stopped, replaced by *slurpy* noises. I smiled to myself as I plugged my dick back into Megan's mouth. Our brief break – all the fault of my thumb, of course – was over and it felt good to be finally getting back to work.

Chapter 30

"Okay girls," I said, "before we go on, tell me one more time. What's the number one rule going forward?"

With grins on their faces, Megan and Jamie chanted, in unison, "No. Dick. Biting." Then they cracked up, rolling around on the bed, laughing. And with that out of the way, we went back to work.

"So, ... how're we gonna do this anyway?" Joey said as we finished up fucking both girls while they were sixty-nining it. It was time to move to the scenes that would be the main part of the video – of each girl's video. Buttfucking.

"Well, I need to be able to split the footage we get tonight into two videos, so I was thinking we'd do it like this. We'll start with both of the girls on the bed, on their hands and knees, with us fucking them doggy style, side by side."

"In the pussy, right?"

"Yup."

"Who fucks who?"

"Doesn't make any difference. Halfway through we're gonna switch girls and film the exact same sequence again."

"Okay, I wanna fuck Jamie first."

"What did you just say?" Meg asked him, her voice menacing. It was difficult to tell whether she was serious or just kidding around. But if she was serious, you didn't want to mess with her – she was famous, or perhaps *infamous*, for her temper.

Joey coughed up a nervous chuckle. "Saving the best for last, sweetie," he said, offering her an anxious smile to go along with his explanation.

"You'd better say something like that," she told him. But she was grinning as she said it, indicating she'd just been yanking Joey's chain.

"Okay. So I'll set up the big camera to catch both of us cuntfucking them at the same time. Then I'll grab my camcorder and film just you and Jamie for a minute or two. And then I'll hand the camcorder to you so you can do the same – film me fucking Megan, up close. We'll be side by side so it'll be easy."

"You gonna let the big camera keep running?"

"Yeah, I'll edit out any stuff we don't want and add in the footage we shoot with the camcorders."

"Okay, that sounds good," he said.

"Wait, there's more. *Then*, ... we switch girls and film the same thing we just did with the new girl – you with Meg and me with Jamie. And at the end, we'll ditch the camcorders so we get a nice big-camera shot of the four of us again, only this time we'll be with a different girl than we started with."

"When are you gonna fuck us in the ass?" Jamie said. "That's what we're supposed to be doing, isn't it?"

I grinned at her. "Patience, sweetie. You didn't let me finish. As soon as we finish what I just described, we're gonna repeat the exact same sequence, only this time it'll be buttfucking instead of cuntfucking. You okay with that?"

"I think so. And that's it? Then we're done?"

Megan laughed and answered Jamie's question for me. "Not by a long shot."

"So, ... what? Other positions?"

"Yeah, some of that, for sure. And, ... have you ever done two guys at the same time?"

"Of course I have. Fuck one, suck the other, then switch. I've been doing it with these two guys every Tuesday for the past month."

Meg shook her head. "No, that's not what I mean. Did you ever *fuck* two guys at the same time?"

"What? Fuck two guys?" Jamie looked confused at first but then grinned. "Oh. You mean front and back, right? Double penetration?"

"Exactly. So, have you ever done that?"

"No. I haven't," she said, shaking her head.

"Yeah, well, since there are two guys here and two guys means there are two dicks, I suspect that after tonight you'll be able to answer to answer that question by saying, 'Oh sure, I've done that.'"

"Ohhh, –"

"You know what they say, Jamie," I said, jumping back into the conversation.

She glanced at me. "Actually, I don't. What do they say?"

"There's a first time for everything."

"Really? You guys are gonna both fuck me at the same time?"

"Well, I hadn't been planning to include that but now that Megan brought it up, it sounds like a good idea. What do you think? You ready for something like that?"

"A dick in my pussy and a dick in my ass? At the same time?"

"Yup."

"Oh boy, oh boy!"

"That doesn't scare you?" Megan said. "Having two gigantic dicks inside you at the same time? One pounding your pussy while the other one pounds your ass?"

"Fuck, no! I've been dreaming about doing nasty stuff like that since I was a little ... since I turned 18."

Meg shook her head. "Talking about it – and dreaming about it – is one thing. We'll see what happens when it comes time to do it. I'll tell ya, it scared the shit outa me the first time I did it. Not literally, of course."

"Really, Jamie?" I said. "You've dreamed about taking on a dick in your front door and a dick in your back door at the same time?"

"Uh-huh. Lots of times. Daydreams, mostly – wondering what it would feel like, whether it would hurt or not, how good it would feel, what an orgasm would feel like. Stuff like that. But just since I turned 18, you know. Since I saw a girl in a porn video doing it."

"Of course. In these dreams, your daydreams, how did it feel? Did you like it?"

She giggled. "Fuck, yeah! It felt *wonderful!*"

It was my turn to shake my head. "Well, that particular dream could become a reality here tonight. So, ... if I fuck your ass while Joey fucks your pussy at the same time, you're down with that?"

"Oh boy, oh boy," she said.

"Okay, then. I'll take that as a *yes*. Let's get started."

Chapter 31

It was after nine o'clock by the time Joey and I wrapped up our *warm-up* activities and were ready to get started on the main event of the evening, fucking both girls in the ass. While everything we'd done so far had gone smoothly, I couldn't help but be a little concerned about Jamie's upcoming performance. While she'd *talked* a good game about taking a big dick up her ass, she hadn't actually done that yet. I probably should have auditioned her for that in private, when she'd been staying at my apartment, to see if she could handle a dick my size. But I hadn't.

And then there was Megan, whose normally sweet and shy exterior actually hid a raging, big-cock-worshipping fuckbunny who lurked inside. I was never worried about her. I knew she could handle anything having to do with her ass and big dicks. After all, she was Bonny B. Goode, the Buttfuck Queen of the West, on Fukknumzie. A buttfuck specialist, more or less. Plus, I'd already fucked her in the ass more times than I could count and I knew that Joey routinely buttfucked her at home, too. When they weren't busy pissing on each other, I assumed.

And as for those double penetration scenes that might be included in the upcoming fun, well, I knew Meg would be fine with doing them. I'd have to wait and see how things went with Jamie, though. Hopefully, she'd been practicing with that thick dildo she'd mentioned – using it in her ass, not just in her pussy. And if she could take the assfucking I was planning to give her – without crying or screaming or complaining – then Joey and I would use her in some DP scenes, as well.

Actually, according to a couple of girls with whom I've discussed this, getting fucked in both holes at the same time wasn't as difficult nor as uncomfortable as it might appear to a viewer of the scene. The trick, apparently – if you can even call it a *trick* – was entirely related to a girl's comfort level with having a big dick planted in her ass. If she could handle that for an extended period of time, then adding another big dick to her cunt wasn't that big a deal.

At least, that's what they'd claimed. Both girls who'd told me that. You'd think that at the very least, though, there'd be some uncomfortable *stretching* involved. Wouldn't there? But what the fuck do I know? I'm a guy.

Whatever, it was time to find out how all this was going to play out. To see if Jamie could live up to the claims she'd been making. To discover whether the experience of getting dicked in the ass would later be described by her as "Oh boy, oh boy!" or "Oh no, Oh no!"

"Okay, Jamie, you're up first," I told her.

"Me?" she said, for the first time sounding just a little bit nervous. That might have been because she was a rookie performing under the watchful eyes of a buttfuck pro but I didn't think so. I thought that, for the first time, Jamie was realizing that getting fucked in the ass by a dick attached to a live human male – me – might not be exactly the same as sticking her trusty ten-incher up there. Not only was my dick bigger than her dildo and most likely a *lot* more active, she would no longer be in control of how it acted, how fast it thrust, how deep it plunged – none of that. Everything she controlled when she was using her dildo was now up to me. And it scared her. You could see it on her face.

"Yup. Get up on the bed. Hands and knees. We're gonna start in doggy style."

She cast a nervous glance at the bed and just stood there, not moving for several seconds. Then she pulled her hair back behind her head, holding it as if she couldn't make up her mind whether to wrap a scrunchy around it and turn it into a ponytail or just let it fall down behind her shoulders. Megan, watching with Joey from the sidelines, clapped her hands and said, "C'mon. You got this, girl!" No doubt buoyed by Meg's encouragement, Jamie dropped her hair and climbed up onto the bed and assumed the position I'd requested.

"You just gonna stick it right in my ass, Jumbo?" she said, twisting her head and shoulders around and watching me as I moved into position behind her. "No warm-up?"

I patted her on the ass. "Don't worry, sweetie, I'll warm you up a bit, first, with a little pussy fucking, then I'm gonna use my thumb to loosen up your asshole. Wouldn't want to cause any damage when I plug Junior in, you know."

"Damage? What kind of damage are you talking about?" She looked alarmed.

Damn! That was a mistake. Mentioning that word. I debated whether or not to tell her the truth – that some girls actually bleed when Junior rips through their assholes for the first time. But I decided that would unnecessarily scare her, that lying was a better option.

"Bad choice of words. I meant *pain.* I wouldn't want to cause you any *pain* when I plug him in," I told her.

"Yeah, as if that was a big difference," she mumbled, turning back to the front. "Okay, I'm ready whenever you are."

"Spread your legs a little bit." I tapped the inside of her thigh and when she widened her stance, I slid my hand up to her pussy, slipping in my middle finger for a quick finger fuck. As it seemingly always was, Jamie's pussy was wet. Really, really wet.

She shivered. "Mmm, that feels good. Let's do that, instead."

"Don't get carried away. This is just a moisture check," I said, suppressing a laugh.

"Mmm. You don't have to check me – I'm permanently moist."

Actually, I already knew that. "Joey, you ready?" I asked him. He and Megan were sitting together in an armchair, playing with each other's private parts while they watched Jamie and me.

He picked up a camcorder and climbed out of the chair. "Whenever you guys are."

"Megan, why don't you grab a camcorder, too, and shoot some footage?" I suggested.

"Yeah, okay." She bounced up out of the chair. "Just wander around and shoot stuff from various angles?"

"Exactly. Just do the same as Joey. I'm gonna film it, too – POV – which means I'll have to lean back a little while I fuck her, in order to get a good view. So there'll be plenty of room to shoot from the side, get some closeups or whatever. Just make sure to aim down so you don't get Joey in the shot."

"Okay. Got it."

"So, everybody ready?" I said.

Everyone was ready.

"Then, ... let's fuck."

Chapter 32

Jamie's pussy winked back at me as I lined my dick up behind it. "Lean down a bit," I told her. "Put your elbows down on the mattress."

She did as I asked and when she did, I noticed her pussy was shaking, or vibrating, or *something* – shivering, maybe, as if it was cold. I'd seen it happen to her a couple of other times, too, but it was a little weird. I'd never seen any other pussy – and I've seen a *lot* of them – do that. Only Jamie's. Trembling in anticipation, I guess you'd call it.

"Okay, Jamie. Here we go," I said.

"Oh boy, oh boy!" came her familiar reply.

I slipped my dick into her tight, juicy pussy. Just a couple of inches. Then I paused to give her a chance to adjust. Almost always, when I plant those first two inches or so in a girl's cunt, I get the same reaction. The girl jerks a bit and says, "Unhh!"

But not Jamie. She didn't jerk and she didn't say, "Unhh!" She said, "Mmmmm." Then she turned around and looked at me and added, "Why did you pause?"

"Sorry. Tell me if you want me to stop," I said, feeding her another couple of inches. Nothing happened – she didn't ask me to stop – so I continued pushing forward.

"Mmmmm," was her only comment as Junior continued slowly advancing. She said it several times.

Eventually, my thighs bumped up against her ass and I was forced to stop. Junior was fully planted. "Everything good?" I asked her.

"Better than good. Excellent."

"Okay. I'm gonna pump your pussy for a minute or so, then I'll stick my thumb in your ass and work it around a bit, loosen up your asshole so it won't hurt so much when Junior punches into you."

"Don't worry, Jumbo. I can handle it. I told you – I've been practicing. But warn me about the thumb, will ya?"

"Yeah, I'll do that. Wouldn't want you to bite your tongue or something." I leaned back a bit, aimed my camcorder down at where my dick was connected to Jamie's pussy, and turned it on. "And away we go, Stella," I said, remembering to use her porn name.

"Oh boy, oh boy!" she said.

I'd been expecting her to say that but a smile crossed my face, anyway. And then I did exactly what I'd told her I'd do – I pumped her cunt for a minute or two. When I felt I had enough footage of that, I warned her, "Thumb coming up, Jamie."

"Okay, I'm ready," she said. "Stick it in." Then, in a softer voice no doubt intended just for herself, she added, "Oh boy!"

Leaving my dick temporarily parked deep in her pussy, I pushed my thumb into her ass. I really expected to get that nearly ubiquitous "Unhh!" reaction when I plunged through her asshole. And I did. She said it – "Unhh!" – and she even jerked just a bit. But she followed that up almost immediately with, "Mmmmm."

Her asshole was tight. Most assholes were, at least in the beginning, but a visit from my thumb usually encouraged them to loosen up a bit. And Jamie's backdoor was no exception.

I started with slow, straight thumbfucking, just sliding in and out in a nice, smooth, *easy* motion. Then I added a little twisting motion, leaving my thumb fully planted while I rotated my hand and pushed sideways against the tightness of her asshole in an attempt to enlarge it. Down at the other end, Jamie moaned and uttered her favorite phrase multiple times.

Because my right hand was busy preparing for my dick's grand entrance, I was forced to hold my camcorder in my left hand in order to shoot the scene the way I wanted, looking down, POV. But in spite of my best efforts to keep the action in frame, I couldn't, ending up with shots of the bed and the floor along with only occasional shots of my intended target – my thumb poking Jamie's asshole. As usual, my left hand turned out to be pretty much worthless for camera work.

Eventually, I abandoned the effort, tossed my camcorder onto a nearby chair, and called over Megan, who was filming a side view of the action.

"What?" she said, watching my thumb.

"I need you to lean over in front of me and shoot some footage. POV. Keep your camcorder sideways so it'll look like I shot the scene and aim it straight down. Hold it right about here." I patted the front of my chest.

"Okay. Right now?"

"Yup."

She leaned forward and began shooting. As she did – and out of habit, I guess – I reached behind her, slid my left hand up the inside of her thigh, and using just the index-finger edge, gave her a shark-fin pussy swipe. While my left hand may not have been steady enough for camera work, it seemed to work just fine for locating and stroking pussy.

"Hey! I'm working, here," she said, jumping back and laughing. "Stop it. Save that shit for when it's my turn to sit on Junior."

"Sorry," I said, flashing her my best *not-sorry* grin. "I thought you were *that* kind of girl."

She stuck her tongue out at me and got back into position. "Fuck you, Jumbo."

"You'll get your chance," I told her.

"Oh boy, oh boy," she said, mimicking Jamie.

"How about you, sweetie?" I turned my attention back to the beautiful young girl currently kneeling in front of me with my dick parked in her pussy and my thumb poking her ass. "You okay?"

"Uh-huh. Things are good. Real good." She added a *happy* shake of her butt for emphasis.

"Well, things are about to get better," I told her. I *hoped* that was true – hoped that when I swapped out my thumb for my dick, Jamie would perceive that as being *better* and wouldn't end up crying and screaming about how much pain she was experiencing.

"You mean, ...?"

"Yup. That's what I mean. You ready?"

"What about lube?" she said. "You gonna grease me up?"

"Nope. Here at the *Jumbo Johnson Buttfuck Academy*, we teach our students the truth – you don't need that fancy, expensive, commercial shit. The best lubes come built in. Spit and pussy juice. That's all you need."

She giggled. "So now you're a school?"

"Yup. And I'm your teacher."

"Oh. Well, ... okay then, Mr. Johnson, I'm ready for my lesson. Let's do it."

Chapter 33

As I lined my dick up on Jamie's cute little puckered patootie, I really had no idea of what to expect. And yeah, yeah, I know – that was a big mistake on my part. Truthfully, I couldn't believe I'd let things progress this far without finding out how she'd react to having a dick – a really big dick – repeatedly shoved up her ass.

I mean, I knew she *talked* a good game. She claimed she *knew* how to do it and that she'd been practicing at home with her big fat dildo. She said she *wanted* to do it. But so far, she'd never actually *done* it with a real live dick. At least, not that I'd seen or been a part of. So far, it had been all talk and no action. And now all that was about to be put to the test.

I mentally crossed my fingers, offered up a quick plea to the fuck gods for a good reaction, then drooled a big gob of spit down onto Jamie's butt crack and watched as it raced down to her asshole. When it got there, I spread it around and pushed some inside. Junior was already nicely coated in her slippery pussy juice and was eager to get back inside something – *anything* – and resume fucking.

"Hand me my camcorder," I said to Megan.

She gave it to me and moved out of the way as I aimed it down at Jamie's wet, glistening asshole.

"Okay. Ready or not, here we go, sweetie."

"I'm ready," Jamie said. "Do it."

"I'm gonna count to three and on the count of three I'll push Junior in, just a little ways, maybe a couple of inches. Okay?"

"Sure."

"Try to relax," I said, offering her some last-minute advice.

"I *am* relaxed." She turned around and looked at me. "You're the one who seems nervous. Maybe *you* should relax."

I chuckled but she was right. She seemed pretty calm and relaxed about what was going to happen. *I* was the one exhibiting the signs of nervousness.

"I'll be fine," she said, turning back around and wiggling her ass at me in a playful manner. "Just do it."

"Okay. On three, then." I rested my dickhead on her asshole and prepared to thrust. "One. Two. And –" But I never made it to three because at the two-and-a-half mark, Jamie slammed her ass backward and impaled herself on my dick.

"*Three!*" she said, adding a giggle. "There. That wasn't so bad, was it?"

I couldn't help but laugh, both in amazement and with relief. There had been no screams, no cries of pain, not even an "Unhh!" as Junior punched into her. Nothing. Just silence. "You're amazing, Jamie," I told her.

"I know. That's what all the guys say."

"What? What guys?"

"Uh, ... in my dreams. That's what all the guys in my dreams say. They tell me I'm amazing."

"Well, those guys are right. You *are* amazing."

"Thank you, Jumbo," she said. "Now please – please, please, please! – show me what you've got."

It was hard to refuse a girl who said please, who actually *begged* to have her ass fucked. So I showed her. I slowly worked my dick farther into her, stopping when about half of Junior was comfortably seated. "How's that feel?" I asked her.

"You want the truth?"

"Of course I do."

"It, ... well, it kinda feels like I gotta poop."

My response to that was laughter.

"Is that weird?" she said.

"Nope. Not at all. That's pretty much what all the girls say."

"Oh. Okay, then, ... good."

"So, no pain or anything?"

"No pain," she said. "It's good. I feel full, you know. Really full. And, ... and just *good*."

"All right, then. Let's continue." I leaned back a little in order to capture a good view of the action and began to slow-pump her ass, planting my dick a little deeper with each stroke.

This was the part where some girls have problems. Taking Junior deep, I mean. I can always tell by the signs of *distress* coming from up front. The crying, the screaming, the creative swear words, and the escape attempts are just some of the clues they're uncomfortable with what has been described to me – more than once – as 'like having a telephone pole jammed up my butt.'

Not Jamie, though. No screams or cries came from her. She knelt quietly as I rocked back and forth, pushing deeper and deeper, until finally she said, "Mmmmm, that feels really good. I like it. Fuck me, Jumbo. Fuck me good!"

So that's what I did. I fucked her good. Or at least, I *tried* to, picking up speed and slamming her ass while I struggled to hold my camcorder steady and on target and thanked the fuck gods for the invention of image stabilization.

Almost immediately – I hadn't poked her ass more than eight or nine times, I swear – Jamie had an orgasm. Actually, a series of them would be a more accurate description. Maybe a half dozen or more, spaced about 10 seconds apart. Not *big* orgasms, just small, less intense mini-orgasms is what they were, I guess. None of those wild, fish-flopping-around-the-bed, Big-O type orgasms she'd shown us before – she'd merely pause for a few seconds while her butt and her legs shook violently and her fingers clawed at the sheet beneath her. Then she'd return to slamming her ass backward onto my dick, moaning and throwing in an occasional "Oh boy!" or two in a soft voice. Evidently, all that practice she'd been doing since she'd turned 18 was paying off.

I got the distinct feeling that when Fukknumzie fans saw Jamie's videos – especially this one – it was going to pay off for her there, as well. Big time.

Chapter 34

"Oh, oh, oh! Fuck me, Jumbo. Fuck me *hard!*" Jamie begged me.

I'd been pumping her ass for several minutes and she was beginning to show signs of another approaching orgasm. A big one, this time. Maybe even that fish-flopping Big O. "Are you gonna cum again?" I said.

"Uh-huh."

"A biggie?"

"If I were a gambler, I'd bet on it." She slammed her ass backward. Hard.

"Don't," I told her.

"Don't? Don't cum?"

"Yeah."

"But I *wanna!*" She stopped her backward slamming, turned her head, and frowned at me.

I stopped, too. "You and me both. But you're a pro now, Jamie. We're making a video and you can't always do what you *wanna*. You've gotta learn to delay your orgasms."

"Well, fuck!" she said. "That's no fun."

"Yeah, tell me about it," I said, chuckling. She was right. Not being able to cum when you wanted to – *really* wanted to – was a major drawback of being a porn actor. "Anyway, I've got a treat in store for you that'll make you glad you waited."

"You do? What is it?"

"It's a surprise."

"Oooohhh, a surprise, huh?" She paused briefly, maybe trying to figure out what it might be. Then, with just a hint of concern in her voice, she added, "You're not gonna try to ... fuck my ear, are you?"

"Hmm, fuck your ear, huh? That's not actually what the surprise is, ... but now that you mention it, ... hmm."

"Forget it. You know I was kidding."

I grinned at her. "You sure? You'd be the only girl on Fukknumzie doing that."

"Pretty sure," she said, bouncing my grin back at me. "So, about that surprise?"

"Are your ears both the same size, sweetie? Or is one of them bigger than the other?" I asked her.

"Stop it!" She reached back and attempted to swat me with her hand but her arm was too short and she slapped her ass, instead. "You fuck me in the ear and I'll have my daddy sue you. C'mon, show me my surprise."

"Okay. One surprise, coming right up. First off, I need you to stand up."

"Stand up? On the bed?"

"I mean stand up on your knees. Straighten up."

"So what you mean is you need me to *kneel* up, right?"

"Yeah, I guess. Whatever. What are you, an English teacher now?"

She shook her head, still grinning at me. "No, but I had a wonderful English teacher last semester. Mr. Glenn. He taught me all kinds of good things."

I wanted to ask her exactly what kinds of *good things* the wonderful Mr. Glenn had taught her but before I could, she turned back to the front, *knelt* up, and said, "Okay, what's next?"

I handed my camcorder to Joey, telling him to move my big camera to the side and get into position at the edge of the bed. Then I reached around Jamie, cupping both breasts and tweaking her nipples with my fingers. "You've got really nice tits, sweetie," I whispered in her ear.

"That's it?" she said. "That's the big surprise? Playing with my boobs and pinching my nipples?"

"Nope, that's not it. Lean back a little, so that you're resting against me."

"Why?"

"Don't ask. It's part of the surprise. Just do it."

She shook her head and said, mostly to herself, "What now?" But she leaned back against me, wiggling her ass at the same time and making Junior, still plugged in and waiting patiently for action to resume, stir in anticipation.

I slid my hands from her tits down to her thighs and hooked them behind her knees. "Hang on," I told her. "We're gonna go for a little ride." Then I straightened up, lifting her until she was suspended in the air in front of me, supported by a tripod of a hand beneath each knee and my dick in her ass.

"Ooooh, don't drop me," she said.

"Never." I turned and headed for the edge of the bed.

"Wheeeeee. This is fun," she said as I knee-walked her over to where Joey stood waiting. But when she saw him standing there, stroking his dick and eyeing her cunt, her tone changed from gleeful to apprehensive. "Oh, oh. Is this it?" she asked me.

"It?"

"My surprise? You guys are gonna DP me?"

"Yeah, that's the plan. You good with that?"

"I guess. Is it gonna hurt? Tell me the truth – don't lie to me."

"It might, if you've never done it before. I don't suppose you've got *two* giant dildos at home so you could practice this, do you?"

"No, I don't."

"So yeah, it might hurt. There's obviously some stretching involved and that might be a little, ... uncomfortable."

"Well, you know my nickname," she said, laughing. "I'm Stretch Topin, so I oughta be okay."

I laughed, too, then told her, "Nice line, Jamie, but I'm gonna have to cut it out. I'm afraid someone will figure out your real identity. And that line won't make any sense to viewers of the video, anyway, since the only name they'll know by is Stella."

She shrugged. "Whatever."

Joey stepped closer. "Hey, you guys just gonna keep talking or are you gonna let me get in on this little love fest?"

"Boy oh boy, somebody's eager to destroy my pussy," Jamie said.

Joey laughed. "I'm not gonna hurt your pussy, Stella. I'll be real gentle. I love pussy – that's the only reason I took this job."

Megan, who was standing near Joey, filming the scene with a camcorder, looked up at him and said, "What!! You took this job for the *pussy*?!!"

"And the money. And the money. Mostly for the money," he quickly added. "We needed to save money, remember? So we could buy a house and, ... and, ... you know."

Poor Joey. He sounded frantic, standing there and practically starting to sweat as Megan glared at him. Pussy whipped! It was ridiculous, really. All an act on her part – she was yanking his chain. I was pretty sure she knew that the main thing Joey liked about this job was all the chances he got to fuck beautiful young women like Jamie. Not the money. This was the kind of job most guys would do for free.

"Don't hit him, Meg," I tossed into their conversation. Just for fun.

"I'm not gonna," she said.

"Well, don't scare him, either. Look. His fucking hard-on's starting to droop."

She looked, then fixed Joey with a smile that could only be described as *evil-looking*. "Want me to fluff Little Joey back up for you, honey?" she said to him in a super-sugary-sweet voice.

A terrified look passed over his face as he stared back at her. "Uh, ... no. I don't think I do."

"Aww, c'mon. Let me suck it for you."

"I don't think so. You're planning to bite me. I can tell. I'll get Jamie to fluff me up." He turned to face Jamie, still suspended in the air in front of him, her legs spread wide. Stretch Topin, one might say, if one were in a joking mood.

"I don't think my mouth can reach your dick from up here," she told him. "And besides, I'm, uh, ... kinda busy doing something else right now, you know?"

That was true. Jamie *was* otherwise engaged. At the time, she was busy squirming around on my dick in an attempt to keep Junior – and herself – entertained.

"Fine. I'll do it myself," he said.

Megan looked at Jamie.

Jamie looked at me.

I looked at Megan.

All three of us looked at Joey.

He stood in front of Jamie's spread legs, staring at her wet, inviting pussy with an angry expression on his face, furiously stroking his dick in an effort to resurrect the hard-on Megan had evidently sent to the great beyond.

And then the entire room – with the exception of Joey – burst into laughter.

Chapter 35

"You're on roving camera duty, Megan. Okay?"

She nodded. "I'm ready."

"Joey?"

"Yeah, I'm ready, too." He waved his dick around, showing us he'd been able to fluff it back into *performing* shape using only his hand. Of course, that wasn't really a great feat of magic or something only Joey could do. Just about any guy with at least one hand could use that hand to make his dick hard. Still, he seemed kind of proud of himself.

"All right, then. Let's do this." I lifted Jamie's legs a little higher and pulled them even farther apart, presenting her pussy to Joey at the best possible angle for easy penetration.

He stepped forward and began sliding his now nicely firmed up dick back and forth along her juicy slit, just inside her labia, without inserting it.

"Mmmmm, that feels good. Let's just keep doing that," she suggested.

"What I have in mind feels even better, sweetie. How do you want it?"

"What? Whaddaya mean?"

"How do you want me to plug it in? Fast or slow?"

She didn't answer.

"Jamie?" he said. "I mean, ... Stella?"

"Yeah, I'm thinking. Which way is better?"

"Well, for me, just jamming it in quickly is the way to go. But for you, I don't know. It's kind of a personal preference."

She stopped wriggling on my dick and appeared to think about it, finally deciding, "I guess I'd prefer slow, if that's good with you."

"Not a problem." He gripped the shaft of his dick firmly, lined up his dickhead, gave her pussy a couple of good-luck wipes with his dickhead, and lined the tip up with her entrance. "Okay, here we go," he said.

"Slowly," she reminded him.

"Hold her tight," he said to me. Then he pushed forward, quickly driving about three inches of his dick into her cunt, and paused, waiting to see what would happen.

Jamie's reaction was immediate. And loud. "Unhh! Owww! Fuck!" she called out to the world. "You call that *slow*?"

"Sorry. Your pussy's so tight, punching in slowly is impossible. But I'll feed the rest of my dick to you nice and slow, I promise."

"I'm having second thoughts about this," she said. "I think maybe agreeing to do this was a mistake on my part."

"Just relax, Jamie," I whispered in her ear. "Once Joey gets his dick all the way in, things will start to feel good."

"Yeah, good for you guys, I'm sure. But for me, ...?"

"It'll feel good to you, too. C'mon. You know you want this. You've been dreaming about doing nasty stuff like this ever since you turned 18, right?"

"Yeah, I know, but dreams and reality are not exactly the same thing. I never thought I'd ever really be doing something like *this* – suspended in the air with a giant dick *way* up my ass while another giant dick is attempting to crawl up my pussy."

"Welcome to the wonderful world of double penetration," I told her. "And we're just getting started."

"Fuck!"

"So, ... are we good to continue?" Joey said.

"Do I have a choice?"

"Well, yeah, you do," I said. "Don't forget, this is *your* video. We're doing what you said you wanted to do."

"I never said anything about DP. That was your idea."

She had me there – it *had* been my idea. "Okay. Maybe so. We can quit if you want, but do you remember why I suggested it?"

"So you two could get freaky with my private parts?"

"No. That wasn't it."

"Then I forget. Why?"

"To make you a star on Fukknumzie. To make you a lot of money."

"Oh, yeah. I *do* want that, you know."

I lifted her up a bit and let her slide back down my dick, getting an 'ooooh' in return. "Just think about all the money you're gonna make, about how popular you're gonna be on that website. Not many girls are doing double penetration."

"But I'm one of them," Megan said, raising her hand.

I looked over at Megan, standing off to the side, her camcorder trained on Jamie's crotch. "She is," I told Jamie. "And she's making a fortune with her videos. Right, Meg?"

"Yup. I'm doing pretty good."

"So a little pain and discomfort now will pay off big time in the future."

"I'm not feeling any pain," Jamie said. "And I'm not actually all that uncomfortable, either."

"Really? Weren't you just screaming in agony a minute ago?"

"Yeah, but that was when Joey was sticking it in. Now that he's inside me, it doesn't hurt. It just feels kinda, ... kinda, ..."

"Kinda what?"

"Snug."

I couldn't help it – I laughed. "Snug, huh? So ...?"

"Might as well keep going, I guess. But this is such an awkward position. Isn't there some other way we can do this?"

"This is just a starting position, sweetie. After this I'm gonna lie back with you on top of me and Joey on top of you and then we'll end up with Joey on the bottom while you straddle him and I fuck your ass doggy style. You won't be stuck up in the air for much longer."

"So? We good to resume?" Joey said.

Jamie nodded and said, "Yeah. But go slow, okay?"

"Slow it is." He began pushing his dick deeper into Jamie's pussy. Slowly. "How's that feel?" he said.

"So far, so good."

"How about you, Jumbo? Can you feel it, too? Can you feel Little Joey sliding into her?"

"Yeah, I can," I said.

"How's it feel? Good? Do you like it? Just wait 'til I start pumping, Jumbo. That's gonna feel *really* good. You're *really* gonna like that."

Megan started laughing and I said, "Fuck you, Joey. Stop improvising dialogue and do what you're supposed to do. Fuck her pussy."

Joey joined in the laughter. "One fucked pussy, coming right up."

Jamie shuddered and said, "Oh boy, oh boy!"

I shook my head, knowing she was going to say that.

Chapter 36

"Oh, boy! *Oh fucking boy!*" Jamie said as orgasm number 40 swept over her, making her shiver all over and causing her legs and ass to shake uncontrollably. Just an approximation, that number – I wasn't actually counting. Might have been 60, for all I knew.

None of those 40 or 60 orgasms were of the *major* variety but Jamie was the queen of mini-orgasms. I'd never seen – or even heard of – any female who could cum that many times in a couple of hours. It was unbelievable. Like a superpower.

And damn! What I wouldn't give for *that* superpower, the ability to cum dozens of times in just a few hours. I'd probably lose a hundred pounds and die of fatigue in about six weeks but, ... damn!

Joey and I had already double-dicked Jamie while she was suspended in the air and while she played the part of the filling in a meat sandwich, with me on the bottom and him on the top. We were just getting started on our final position – Joey on the bottom, her riding his dick like a cowgirl while I fucked her ass doggy style. And Jamie was handling it better than most MILFs with 20 years of experience in the business. For an 18 year old, she was amazing. Absolutely fucking amazing!

"How we holding up, sweetie?" I asked her as I slid my dick deep into her ass. This was my first chance at top position. The earlier times when I'd been underneath her weren't really the best position for buttfucking. But now that I was on top – actually, I was kneeling behind her – I was taking full advantage of it, repeatedly plunging my dick as far up her ass as it would go. "Everything okay?"

Her reply – "Mmmmm." – told me she was doing just fine, that almost an hour of getting both her ass and her cunt fucked by two giant dicks hadn't caused her any serious problems, ... so far. Of course, tomorrow was going to be a different story. She'd be lucky if she could walk. For now, though, things were good, so I grasped her by the hips for better leverage and increased my pumping speed.

"Move your hand," Megan said. "You're blocking my view."

"Whoops, sorry." I pulled my hand back. "Give me that other camcorder. I wanna get some of this POV."

She handed it to me. I leaned my upper body back as far as I comfortably could and held the camcorder out in front of me, attempting to keep it steady as I aimed it down and rocked my lower body back and forth, plugging Jamie's ass at a moderate speed. As I did, it occurred to me I hadn't felt any movement from Joey, recently.

"Hey, Joey, you still alive down there?" I said.

"Shuff berry," came a muffled reply. At least, that's what it sounded like he said.

I leaned forward and to one side so I could see him and immediately spotted the reason for Joey's smothered speech. He and Jamie were kissing. It looked as if they were enjoying it, too. Quite a bit, actually.

Megan seemed to have noticed what they were doing, as well. She'd put her camcorder down and was standing there, her hands on her hips, watching them and shaking her head. She turned to me and pointed – first at me and then back at herself. Then she looped the forefinger and thumb of her left hand together into a circle and inserted the forefinger of her right hand into that circle, sliding it back and forth. Apparently she was unhappy with what Joey was doing and was offering me a revenge fuck as a way to get back at her boyfriend.

I could understand why Megan was upset. I mean, fucking other women and eating their pussies and letting them suck you off was one thing – it was was what porn actors did. But kissing them like you were really, *really* enjoying it? That was a no-no. Although I understood where Joey was coming from – I'd done the same thing with a few of our clients.

And was I up for that revenge fuck Meg had offered me? You bet I was. Megan was a first-class fuck and always gave me a good ride. But since we were *working*, I tucked that away in my *raincheck* file and pinched Jamie's butt, getting a loud, "Owww!" in reply.

She turned her head and gave me a dirty look. "What was that for?"

"Stop kissing Joey," I told her. "We're making a porn video, not a romance movie."

"But I needed something to suck on and Joey's tongue was, ... convenient."

I shook my head. "And Joey, are you working or just having a good time down there?"

"Is that a trick question?"

"No."

"Uh, ... *both*?"

"Well, try to work more and enjoy yourself less. Okay?"

"Yeah, sure," he said.

I felt movement return to Jamie's pussy, beneath me, and my concentration returned to what I was doing. I understood what had occurred down there beneath me – Joey and Jamie had gotten carried away. It happened sometimes due to the nature of what we were doing. And I wasn't immune to it, either. It happened to me, as well.

Yup, you had to keep your head in the game. Concentrate on what you were *supposed* to be doing. Not enjoy yourself *too* much. Do it the way I was currently doing it – fucking Jamie's ass at a moderate speed because that looked good on video when what I really wanted to do was just pinch up a hunk of butt cheek in each hand, pound her ass like there was no tomorrow, and fill her up with tons of cum.

A minute or so after breaking apart the two lovebirds beneath me, Jamie began to shiver and I knew she was about to pop again. I buried my dick deep in her ass and paused, waiting for her 41st – or 61st – spasming orgasm to overtake her. The shivers morphed into full-body trembling.

"Oh fuck!" she said. "Oh fuck, oh boy, ohhh! Ohhhhhhh!"

I waited. These mini-orgasms didn't usually take long.

"Don't stop. Fuck me, Jumbo. Fuck my ass."

Although this particular orgasm seemed to be lasting a little longer than most. As she'd requested, I resumed fucking her ass.

"Fuck me! Fuck me! Fuck me *hard!*" she screamed, slamming backward against my dick.

Yup, this one was a lot longer. And trembling had been replaced by shaking. Serious shaking.

"Ohhhhhhh, fuuuu-uuuck! Oh boy, oh boy! It's a biggie!" she cried.

I handed my camcorder to Megan and grabbed hold of Jamie's hips, pumping her hard and telling her, "Come on, sweetie. Let it go! Cum for us. Then you'll be finished for the night."

And that's exactly what she did. She let it go, cumming for us. Big time.

Chapter 37

Jamie's final orgasm was a magnificent sight. She tried that fish-flopping routine again as the biggie – AKA the Big O – swept over her. But Joey had her wrapped up tightly, his hands holding her upper body in place while his legs trapped her at the ankles, and all she could really do was bounce wildly up and down.

My dick – Junior – seemed to enjoy that bouncing action. And so did my balls. They sent me a *Request to cum* message. I replied with a *Not yet* memo and kept fucking her ass, holding on as best I could while Jamie's hips and butt did their pogo stick impressions.

Just when I thought she might twerk on my dick forever, Jamie suddenly stopped – probably because she was vibrating so hard it had destroyed her bounce rhythm. She just lay on top of Joey and shook violently. Her legs stiffened and locked straight out behind her, thrusting aside Joey's legs in the process. She held that pose – stiff and shaking – for several seconds, then her body seemed to relax, all at once, and in a very quiet voice she said, "Mmmmm. Oh boy."

"You still plugged in down there?" I asked Joey.

"Sorta."

Wasn't sure what that meant, exactly, but it sounded better than him saying, "No." So I said, "Good," and let the conversation drop. I waited for what seemed like a decent amount of time, then extracted Junior from Jamie's ass without cumming, disappointing both him and my balls because I had to delay my own pleasure until after Megan got her turn being DPed.

"I'm gonna go clean up," I said.

Joey said, "Unhh."

Wasn't sure I knew what that meant, either.

I glanced over at him as I left for the bathroom. Jamie had rolled off him and was lying on her back, beside him, panting and attempting to catch her breath. Megan had ditched her camcorder and had climbed up onto the bed. She was lying on his other side, his wet, sticky, still-hard dick in her hand. "You're up next," I said, pointing at her.

The bathroom here at the new studio was big. Really big. I had just managed to get my balls and my dick over the edge of the vanity, into the sink, and was splashing cool water over them when Jamie came in. She turned on the water in the giant, walk-in shower, adjusted the temperature, then came over and stood behind me, wrapping her arms around my waist and pressing herself against my back.

"Wha'cha doing?" she said, peeking around me.

"Cooling off my dick and balls."

"They're hot?"

"More like, ... overly excited."

She reached down and splashed water onto my dick, helping me. "That's 'cause you didn't cum, you know. That's why Junior's all excited."

"Can't cum until we take care of Megan, though," I told her.

"I'm pretty sure Joey's taking care of Megan, right now," she said. "Although, now that I think about it, it's more like, actually, *she's* taking care of *him*."

"What?" I said. But I didn't get an answer.

Instead, Jamie's left hand reached up and turned off the water in the sink. The fingers of her right hand wrapped around my dick, squeezing it. "Forget them. Come with me," she said, tugging my junk out of the sink and turning me around to face her.

Since Junior and I always go everywhere together, I had no choice but to follow her as she led me into the shower. She turned around and stroked my dick with her hand several times as warm water cascaded over us. Both the water and Jamie's hand felt ... good.

"You know the best way to cool off an excited dick?" she asked me.

"Ice?"

She giggled. "You ever do that? Use ice? Does it work?"

"I don't know," I said, shaking my head. "That was a guess. I've never actually tried it."

"Whatever. The best way isn't ice." She dropped to her knees in front of me, relocated Junior from his pointing-north direction by pulling him downward, and slurped him into her mouth.

Before I could tell her to stop – before I could get even the first word out – I was bombarded with messages from my balls and Junior, urging me to reconsider and not say anything, to let Jamie *do her thing.* I looked down at the beautiful girl kneeling in front of me, water streaming over her face, my dick enveloped by those gorgeous lips and her warm mouth, and felt myself beginning to rock back and forth. I reached behind me and turned off the water – it was making her blink.

Ten seconds later, my hands were locked onto Jamie's head, holding it steady while I face-fucked her – hard. Should I have felt guilty because I was blowing up the rest of the evening's shoot? Because if I did what I was planning to do – dump an evening's worth of delayed cum into her pretty little mouth and down her throat – I wouldn't be able to work for the rest of the session?

Sure. I should have felt guilty.

Did I?

Nope. Not one tiny little bit!

My dick began to throb and my balls sought relief by climbing up closer to my body. Identical messages arrived simultaneously – one from my balls and one from Junior – each of them informing me I was no longer in control, they were now running the show.

As I looked down, watching my dick slide in and out of Jamie's greedy little mouth, three thoughts chased each other through my head – two logical, reasonably good thoughts and a third, bad – very bad – one. *Where was my willpower?* led the way. *I'm supposed to be a professional, a guy who cums on demand, not when he feels like it,* followed closely behind. Those were the good thoughts. And in third place, not far behind the two leaders, was the bad thought – *Fuck it! When you gotta cum, you gotta cum!*

It appeared that third thought was doomed to finish in last place when Jamie did something that changed the outcome of the race, that seemed to goose that third-place thought just enough to propel it past the two front-runners and into first place. Her left hand had been keeping itself busy by massaging my balls while her right hand stayed wrapped around my dick, protecting her throat from excessive penetration. But then she released my balls, slid her left hand up my butt crack, and stuck a finger up my ass.

That was all it took. *Fuck it! When you gotta cum, you gotta cum!* crossed the finish line first, well ahead of those other two thoughts. I stopped moving and planted my dick as deep into Jamie's mouth as she'd allow it to go, just laying it on the back of her tongue as it spasmed and throbbed and spurted what seemed like gallons of cum straight down her throat.

Jamie never moved, never reacted in that drowning-girl fashion I'd experienced with so many other girls, where they'd flop about with panicky looks on their faces, each of them choking and frantically trying to remove their head from the vise-like grip in which I held it. She stayed perfectly still, her finger still up my ass, a calm look on her face as I commented on what was happening.

"Oh! Oh, oh fuck!" I told her, adding, "Ohhhhhh, fuuuuuuuuuuuck!!!" for emphasis. I felt like that pretty much explained everything. And yeah, sure, I know. I'd ruined the rest of the evening's shoot, which should have made me feel bad, but it didn't. In fact, I felt ... *great!* Getting your dick drained will change your opinion about lots of things, you know.

Jamie didn't move for a long time. She just knelt there, looking up at me as my dick wilted in her mouth, crawling backward along her tongue as it shrank. I released her head and when I did, the finger of her left hand said goodbye to my ass and departed. Her right hand loosened around the shaft of my shrinking dick and she pumped it a few times in a *good-to-the-last-drop* effort to drain it completely.

Finally, apparently satisfied she'd done all she could do to *cool off* Junior, she popped to her feet, leaning forward and pressing her breasts against me and cupping my ass with her hands. Then, in her softest, sexiest, most romantic voice, she said, "You need to get some of those spongy rubber bath mats. These tiles are pretty but they're killer on the knees."

I wrapped my arms around her and kissed her forehead. Okay. So maybe Jamie's voice didn't really sound all that romantic. Maybe that part was my imagination.

Chapter 38

"You're a miracle, Jamie, you know that? A fucking miracle." I turned the shower back on and we stood there, holding each other as the water splashed over us.

"Not really," she said. "I'm just a girl who loves dick. Especially *your* dick, Charlie."

"Uh-huh."

She squeezed my ass. "Really. Junior's the best."

"If you say so."

"I do." She paused, glancing up at me. "So, ... we gonna go back to work now?"

That made me laugh. "You know, I'm not really in a *working* mood right now. I'm pretty sure we're finished for the night."

"But what about Megan? You guys didn't do her, yet."

"Yup, that's too bad. But I don't have anything left to *do* her with, thanks to you and, ... you know."

"Poor Megan. I'm sorry, Charlie."

"Fuck, don't be sorry. This was my fault, sweetie, not yours. Anyway, she's always got Joey if she needs an orgasm or two."

She giggled. "Yeah, I guess. Anyway, thinking about what they were doing when I came in here, he probably doesn't have anything left to *do* her with, either."

"There you go. Another reason not to go back to work." I turned the water off and we got out, drying ourselves off with the big, fluffy, yellow towels I'd bought online.

"So, ... does this mean we have to come back for one more session?"

I nodded. "Yup, it does."

"Oh boy, oh boy. Another night with Junior."

"It'll mostly be for Megan, you know."

"Sure. But I'll be here and Junior will be here. I'm sure there'll be, ... *opportunities* for me and him to have some fun."

I didn't doubt that at all. "And it can't be on a Tuesday. Or any other weeknight, for that matter. I've got a new girl starting next Tuesday and all my other nights are filled, too."

"Sooo, ...?"

"Hafta be on a weekend, I guess. Can you make it this Saturday night?"

"Sure. I can make it any night for a chance to play with Junior."

"Good. We'll do it then," I said, tossing my towel toward the hamper but missing. I went over and picked it up, dunking it as if it was a basketball. "You dry? Ready to go?"

"I need to dry my hair," she said, pulling the hair dryer – another recent online purchase – out from beneath the sink and plugging it in. "I'll be out in a little bit."

"Okay. See you out there."

"Five minutes," she said, holding up her hand and showing me five fingers. "My hair's thin – it dries real quick."

"Good." I closed the door behind me and went back into the studio, putting my clothes back on. Megan and Joey were gone – out in the living room having an after-fuck beer and smoke, no doubt. Their clothes were gone, too, which meant we were definitely through for the night. I scooped up Jamie's clothes and took them with me as I left for the living room.

"What are you doing with those?" Megan said when I arrived. As I'd suspected, she and Joey were clothed, sitting on the couch, drinking beer and smoking.

"They're Jamie's clothes," I told her.

"Yeah, I can see that. Why did you bring them out here, though?"

I shrugged, not having a good answer for that.

"You should go give 'em to her so she won't be embarrassed when she walks out here, naked, and we're all wearing clothes."

"Yeah, like that would bother her *soooo* much," Joey said.

He was right about that. Walking back out here, naked, wasn't likely to bother Jamie in the least. Still, ... "Okay, yeah. Good idea. I'll be right back."

When I went back and opened the bathroom door, I found Jamie sitting in the sink, bent over so far her tits were resting on her knees. "What the fuck are you doing, sweetie?" I said, giving her a giant grin.

"Cooling my asshole. It hurts." She grinned back at me.

Her explanation made perfect sense but it made me laugh anyway – I couldn't help it. "Why are you all bent over like that?"

"The faucet was poking me in the back. That hurt, too."

More laughter. "I brought you your clothes," I said, putting them down near her.

"Thanks, Charlie."

"There's some moisturizing lotion under the sink," I told her. "Try that." I closed the door and headed back to the living room, still laughing.

"Where's Jamie?" Megan asked me as I plopped myself down on the couch, next to her, and took a long pull on the beer I'd picked up on a detour through the kitchen. "What's taking her so long?"

"She's a girl," I said.

"What's that supposed to mean?"

"You know. She's a girl – girls are slow in the bathroom."

"Fuck you, asshole," Megan said. But she was laughing as she said it.

Joey took a big hit off the joint they were smoking and passed it to me, skipping over Megan. "So, about the rest of the shoot, ..."

"Don't worry abut it. It's canceled. We're gonna need another session to finish up. It's late, I'm tired, and I'm not in the mood to keep going and try to finish things up tonight." I hit the joint.

He grinned, obviously understanding why I was no longer 'in the mood to keep going.' "Good, good. I'm not really in the mood, either."

"So when, then?" Megan said. "Next Tuesday?"

"No. This is Jamie's last scheduled session. I've got a new girl coming in next week."

"So?"

"Jamie's good with Saturday night. How about you guys?"

Megan glanced at Joey, then looked back at me, apparently having received some sort of psychic communication from him because I didn't hear him say anything and the expression on his face hadn't changed. "Yeah, Saturday's good," she said. "We can do that."

"Great." I took a pull off my beer and a hit off the joint, passing it to Megan just as Jamie came prancing back into the living room, naked, her clothes in one hand and a beer in the other.

Chapter 39

Seeing Jamie standing in front of us, naked, made me laugh. I couldn't help it.

"What?" she said. "What's so funny?"

I pointed at the clothes she was holding in her left hand. "You were supposed to put those on."

She shrugged. "I was hot. I'm always hot after a shower. I'll put them on after I cool off. Is that *okay* with you?"

"Sure. Have a seat," I said, replacing my laughter with a giant smile. I patted the couch.

"Thanks." She flopped down next to me.

"You *are* hot," I told her, noticing the tiny beads of perspiration covering her skin.

"Yeah, that's what all the guys say."

I started laughing again. There was something about Jamie's slightly sarcastic *feigned* innocence that always made me laugh – I could never *really* be sure if she was serious or faking it.

"Move over a little," she said.

I slid over, closer to Megan.

"Not *that* way. Closer to *me*. I wanna cuddle."

"Won't that just make you hotter?" I said.

She smiled up at me as I put my arm around her. "I'm already pretty hot. The only thing that would make me hotter is more makeup," she said, fluttering her eyelashes at me.

"All right, all right," Joey said as he, Megan, and myself all broke out in laughter. "Best line of the night!"

I had to agree. I pulled her closer to me and told her, "You don't need *any* makeup, sweetie. You're the definition of *hot*."

She dropped a hand into my lap and gave my dick a friendly squeeze through the thin material of my shorts. "Thanks, Charlie. You're so sweet."

"Oh, oh," Megan said. "This situation looks like it's about to turn into an orgy. C'mon, Joey. We'd better leave." She stood up and attempted to tug him up after her.

"Leave?" he said, getting to his feet. "Why? What's wrong with an orgy?"

Megan fixed him with a look that could only mean what she'd just said – *we'd better leave*. "I'm tired and I wanna go home, *that's* why."

I thought he might mention that they'd arrived in separate cars and he didn't have to leave just because she wanted to, but he didn't. Which was a really smart move, in my estimation. Instead, he said, "Okay, we'll take your car, then. And you can drop me off tomorrow or I'll grab an Uber."

"Great. Let's go." She turned to us. "See you guys on Saturday, then."

"Yup." I nodded and Jamie squeezed my dick again, as if that was some sort of response.

"You need a ride, Jamie?" Joey said. "Or is your *boyfriend* picking you up again?"

"I'm good," she said, smiling up at him. "But thanks for the offer."

"Then we're outa here, I guess." He took Megan's arm and as they headed for the front door, she waved goodbye to us – just a little three-finger toodle-oo – and said, "See ya Saturday!"

"Drive carefully," I called after them.

As soon as they were gone, Jamie said, "Listen, don't tell Joey 'cause I know it drives him nuts, not knowing, and I like that. But my so-called *boyfriend*, ... well, he's not. He's just an Uber driver."

"Yeah, I suspected as much."

She giggled. "Joey's kind of a mulch, don't you think? I mean, don't get me wrong – I like him and all. He's nice. Megan, too. She's a sweetheart."

"What's a mulch?" I asked her, taking a chug of my beer.

"You know."

"No, actually I don't. What's it mean?"

"It means, ... a little stupid. Naive, maybe? Something like that."

"Okay then, you're right. He's a mulch."

She leaned over and unbuttoned my shorts, pulling the zipper down and sliding her hand inside, scratching my pubes. "You need to trim your pubic hair," she said, her fingers drawing circles in that hairy jungle just above my dick.

"Yeah, I've been meaning to do that."

"Want me to do it for you?"

"My clippers are at my apartment."

"There's scissors in the bathroom. I saw them. I could use those." She gave Junior a squeeze and I felt him stir slightly.

"Sorry, sweetie. Nobody – and I mean, *nobody* – gets near my junk with sharp instruments like scissors."

She giggled. "Really, Charlie? You don't trust me?"

"*I* do. But Junior doesn't trust anyone but me." And then, in an attempt at changing the subject, I said, "Hey, how's your asshole? Feeling better?"

"Yeah, it's okay. I put some of that lotion on it." She began squeezing Junior in a rhythmic fashion, over and over, apparently urging him to wake up.

"What are you doing, Jamie?" I said, nodding down at my lap.

"Nothing. Just keeping busy. Ignore me."

"Easier said than done."

"Yeah." She was silent for a while, watching her hand as it played with Junior. Eventually, she looked up at me and said, "Do you think liking to get fucked in the ass makes me a bad person, Charlie? Getting orgasms from it? Am I weird? Am I a freak?"

"Fuck no, absolutely not. You're not weird. Lotsa girls like it in the butt, not just you. And it has nothing to do with whether you're good or bad."

"Yeah, but other girls – the ones I know, anyway – *don't* like it. Don't do it. I've got girlfriends, you know. You know what they say when we talk about it?"

"Nope. What?"

"Weird shit. Stuff like, 'I'd rather take a rolling pin in the cunt than let a guy stick his cock up there.' And, 'Any guy tries that with me and I'll bite his dick off.'"

"Ouch," I said, laughing.

"And you know the worst? They say no *decent* girl –" She made one-handed air quotes around the word *decent*. "– would ever do that. Only whores, old ladies, and gay guys take it up the butt. But I like it, you know."

"Don't worry about them, Jamie. About what they say. They don't know what they're missing."

"Yeah." She grew quiet again, continuing her dick massage. After a while, she said, "This is just like old times, Charlie. You and me, sitting on a couch, drinking beer and smoking weed. Just like when we used to live together."

"Yup. And you with your hand constantly in my pants, playing with my dick. But we didn't actually live together, sweetie," I said, lightly pinching a nipple as Junior began to stiffen beneath Jamie's fingers. "You just stayed with me for a few days."

"Yeah, I know. But it kinda felt the same. We ate together, we watched TV together – and porn, too. And we slept together."

"Yup. We did. And even though I didn't get much done that week – fuck, I had to cancel sessions and everything – I enjoyed it. I really liked having you stay with me."

"Thanks, Charlie. I liked staying with you, too. And boy oh boy, we sure fucked a lot, didn't we?"

I couldn't argue with that. Fucking *had* been our main activity during those few days she stayed with me. "Yeah, we certainly did. You know, I lost seven pounds that week."

"Seven pounds of cum," she said, laughing.

"Exactly." I pulled her closer to me and gave her a squeeze.

"So look, if you liked having me stay with you, ... and I liked it, too, how about tonight?"

"Tonight?"

"Yeah. How about I go home with you and spend the night?" She leaned over and kissed Junior on the head, turned it into a bit of a French kiss, then looked up at me with an expectant smile on her face.

"You're horny?" I said. "After all the dick you've had inside you tonight, you're *still* horny?"

She shrugged. "What can I say? I like dick."

Chapter 40

Jamie kept her hand in my shorts for the entire ride to my apartment, not really doing much, just holding Junior and giving him an occasional squeeze. But by the time we arrived, he seemed to have forgotten she'd just sucked him off less than an hour earlier. He was stone hard and ready for some serious fucking.

This was such a bad idea. Bringing Jamie, or any of the girls I worked with, home for a night of just-for-fun suckyfucky was just begging for my life to get more complicated. And fuck, didn't I get enough pussy at work? What the fuck was wrong with me, anyway? Why was I doing this?

Why? That was the question on my mind as I unlocked the front door and let us in. But actually, I knew why. It was mainly about enthusiasm – Jamie's enthusiasm for all things sexual.

She loved dicks. Especially big ones. All you had to do was ask her and she'd tell you all about it. And she not only loved dicks, she liked to do things with them. Like, ... try to swallow them. She also liked to stick them in her pussy. And up her butt.

Yup. Lots of girls dreamed about doing nasty stuff with giant dicks, but Jamie was different. She turned her dreams into real-life adventures. And she was very, *very* enthusiastic about those adventures.

Of course, it also helped – greatly – that I was attracted to her. She was young and beautiful and funny and just a naturally sweet person. She sucked cock like it was the best-tasting food in the entire universe. She also had one of the smoothest, tightest pussies Junior had ever visited – not tight because it was too small, like some girls, but tight because the entire length of that wonderful canal kept a really *firm* grip on my dick each time I plunged it into her.

Oh! And as an added bonus, Jamie's pussy had a delicious, fresh, fruity flavor that made it a joy to eat. So yeah, when you got right down to it, I guess I did know why I was bringing Jamie home for some suckyfucky even though I got plenty of that at work.

"You want a beer?" I said, turning on some lights and steering her toward the living room while I detoured into the kitchen, pretty sure she'd say yes. Even if she didn't, I wanted one.

"Sure."

I grabbed two beers and joined her on the living room couch, where she'd already used her knowledge of the not-so-secret location of my stash box and had removed it from its hiding place under the couch.

"You don't mind, do you?" She smiled up at me as she put the box on the coffee table in front of us and held up a joint.

"Nope. Go ahead, light it up." I handed her a beer.

"This is why I don't drive my car to sessions, you know." She fired up the joint, hit it, and passed it to me. "Beer and weed," she explained as she exhaled.

"Afraid you'll get a ticket?" I took a hit.

"Shit, it's not just a ticket, they *arrest* you! Take you down to the station and book you. You have to get someone to bail you out. Fuck! My father would probably shit grapes, he'd be *soooo* pissed at me if I got arrested for drunk driving. Andrea, too."

I could believe that. Especially about Andrea. "Yeah, that would be, ... not good."

"Why do you always sit so far away from me?" she said, sliding closer to me. "Don't you like me?"

I laughed. "I like you just fine, sweetie. Why do you always wanna sit so close to me?"

"It's easier to reach Junior." She giggled, opened the front of my shorts, and slipped her hand inside, calling in a soft, high-pitched voice, "Oh, Junior ... where are you?"

It didn't take Jamie long to locate Junior. While the two of them got reacquainted, I took another hit off the joint and leaned my head back, attempting to hold the smoke in my lungs while I silently counted to 30. Thirty seconds – something I hadn't been able to do recently.

I failed to reach 30, exhaling at 23, but the attempt did produce a nice buzz. My head felt warm and my brain felt, ... thick. And fuzzy. When I looked back down at Jamie and Junior, they were making out. Smooching. Kissing each other, it looked like. I suppose I could have been jealous but for some reason, ... I wasn't. "You guys having fun down there?" I asked her.

"We are," she said, keeping her attention on Junior and not looking at me. "You should join us."

"I *am* sort of involved, already, you know."

"Yeah, I know you guys are like, ... kinda attached and all, but it's not as if Junior's doing a whole lot, you know. *I'm* doing all the work down here."

"Okay, let's go in the bedroom and I'll share some of the workload with you," I suggested. "How's that sound?"

"That sounds *great!*" Apparently eager to get started, she hopped off the couch, hauled me to my feet, and pulled me after her toward the hallway, almost causing me to do a face plant into the coffee table when my shorts fell to my ankles and tripped me. "Clumsy much?" she said, looking back at me and giggling as I struggled to remain upright.

Less than a minute later, I was fully engaged in *sharing the workload* with Jamie. And showing her I wasn't clumsy. That I was, in fact, poised. Graceful, even. And also showing her that I had a long, thick, *educated* tongue.

She lay on her back, her legs spread wide, oohing and ahhing and pulling my hair as I plunged that tongue – educated by years of practice, if you must know my credentials – deep in her pussy while at the same time poking her clit over and over with the tip of my nose. I like to think of that particular technique as *The World-Famous, Jumbo Johnson Nose Job.* Not to be confused with the kind of nose jobs done by plastic surgeons, of course.

And while all this was happening – while my face was buried deep between her legs and it seemed nothing existed other than the fruity taste and heavenly aroma of Jamie's pussy – a thought occurred to me. A revelation. I realized I'd been wrong – *totally* wrong – when I'd thought bringing Jamie home for the night was a bad idea. It wasn't a bad idea. It was a *great* idea!

Chapter 41

In the morning – the *late* morning – Jamie and I went out for a leisurely breakfast. After we ate, I took her home, glad it was the middle of the day and I likely wouldn't have to experience the awkwardness of bumping into Andrea while Jamie was around. The judge was probably in court – as a judge should be – in the process of sentencing some poor slob to a year in the county slammer for letting his dog bark too much. Or some other, similarly heinous crime.

Whatever. I had a shitload of stuff I needed to do. Editing, mostly. Not only for Jamie's footage but for that of several other girls, as well. And there were other things, too, like washing sheets and towels. That was getting to be a major, time-consuming pain in my ass – I'd already decided to hire one of those companies that supply linen services so I wouldn't have to do that anymore. I just hadn't gotten around to it yet. I added it to my mental list of things I needed to get done.

I definitely had a lot to do. And did I get any of those things on my list accomplished? No I did not. Instead, I managed to convince myself I was tired, that I should rest up so I'd be in good shape to *perform* at my Wednesday evening session. All of which was true, of course. Spending the night with Jamie in my bed had not been conducive to getting a good night's sleep.

So I went home, flopped onto my couch, and treated myself to a couple of beers. And smoked some weed. Those turned out to be really clever moves for a guy whose ass was dragging and who had a thousand things to do. Because my breathing became shallow and my eyelids got heavy.

Yup, there was no doubt about it. I was tired. Really, really tired. Pretty much wiped out. But I'm a reasonably intelligent person and I quickly realized there was a solution – an *easy*, readily available solution – to my fatigue problem.

I took a nap.

* * *

The remainder of the week flew by as I devoted my time to catching up on my neglected projects and on Saturday evening, Joey and I got busy wrapping up the scenes for the Jamie-and-Megan combo videos we'd been unable to finish on Tuesday. So far, most of the evening had been devoted to me buttfucking Megan in various positions. Joey wasn't particularly thrilled with the way that had turned out – because Meg was his girlfriend, he thought he should have gotten the ass-master position. But we'd taken a vote and the final tally was two votes – mine and Megan's – for me, while Joey voted for himself and Jamie had abstained. And though he'd tried to get Jamie to change her non-vote to a vote for him, he gave up when I informed him that would result in a tie and I, as the owner of *Jumbo Johnson Productions*, held the tiebreaker.

So Joey had been forced to console himself with fucking Megan's pussy during the double penetration scenes, which, in my humble opinion, was a helluva nice consolation prize. *Very* nice. Except, of course, the two of them lived together and he could tap that fine piece of ass at home just about anytime he wanted to. So maybe for him, it wasn't a prize at all.

Whatever. All that had been successfully ironed out and we were in the process of shooting the final sequence of the night, the big double-cumshot scene that would serve as the ending for each girl's video. The girls were kneeling on the floor, their heads together, looking up at Joey and me as we whacked our dicks, inches above their faces. I'd been getting urgent messages from my balls for the last minute or so, informing me that launch time was rapidly approaching, and I assumed Joey was in a similar situation.

"Come on, girls. Look thirsty," I told them.

Instead of doing that, they giggled. Then giggles turned into laughs – pretty hard laughs, too. And that's when Joey, without any warning, launched his first spurt. Well, he did say, "Whoops!" as that gob of cum went flying through the air, heading in the general vicinity of the girls' upturned faces, but that doesn't count as a warning, does it?

It didn't really matter, anyway. As frequently happens with Joey, that first spurt was completely off target. But as it sailed by their heads and splattered against the wall behind them – barely missing them both – it caught their attention. They remembered what they were supposed to be doing and stopped laughing, opened their mouths and attempted to 'look thirsty.'

And just in time, too, as subsequent jets of cum gushed downward from Joey's dick, at first getting dangerously close to their intended target and then actually hitting it. The sight of his sticky, white fuck-juice splashing onto the girls' faces and into their open mouths seemed to encourage my balls. They issued a shout of joy that only I could hear and began pumping ammunition to Junior, my cum cannon.

My aim was much better than Joey's. None of *my* deliveries were wasted on the wall. I managed to hit noses and chins and foreheads and dump at least half my load into open mouths. By the time I ran out of ammo, both girls looked like survivors of a mayonnaise war.

"I don't believe it," I said as Jamie – looking like she had a milk mustache – reached up and squeezed the last few remaining drops of cum from Junior into her cum-covered mouth.

"Believe what?" Megan said, getting to her feet. "That Joey actually managed to get some cum onto our faces?"

I handed her a towel as I watched Jamie nibble the head of a shrinking Jumbo, Jr., who appeared to be trying to escape the confines of her mouth. "No. Well yes, that's hard to believe, too. But what I meant was that we're finished. All of Jamie's videos and this last one, for each of you, all done. Finally."

"Except for audio overdubs and editing," she said.

"Yeah, but I'm trying not to think about that right now."

"Anyway, Jamie doesn't seem to realize that we're finished." She nodded in Jamie's direction.

"She knows." I glanced back down, watching her as she sucked my dying dick. But just to make certain, I tapped her on the head. "The scene is over, Jamie," I informed her. "You can stop now."

Temporarily abandoning her efforts, she looked up at me and said, "Junior was still leaking, Charlie. And you know what they say."

"What?"

"Waste not, want not." She slurped poor tired, limp Junior back into her mouth, gave him one final squeeze and a *monster* suck, swallowed, then popped to her feet. "Got one of those for me?" she said, nodding at the towel in Megan's hands as cum dripped from her chin, landing on the floor.

I handed her a towel.

"That went great," she said. "That final scene is gonna look *soooo* good in our videos, don't you think?"

"I do," I agreed.

"So, that's it, right? We're finished? *Completely* finished?"

"Yup, that's it. I've got all the footage I need."

"Great." She turned to Megan. "Wanna go take a shower?"

"Together?"

"Sure. Why not? It's a really big shower. Lots of room. I'll wash your back and you can wash mine."

Megan grinned. "That sounds like fun. Okay, let's do it."

I watched as the two of them, holding hands, headed for the bathroom. And I decided that maybe I *didn't* have all the footage I needed. "Hey, Joey," I said.

He looked up as he continued toweling off his balls and his dick. "What?"

"Grab a camcorder and go into the bathroom. Get some shots of the girls washing each other off in the shower. Or whatever they're doing in there. Maybe I'll include some of that in their videos."

He picked up a camcorder and started to leave, saying, "Okay. I can do that."

"And Joey?"

"Yeah?"

"You don't have to let them play with your junk, you know. We're off the clock. Jamie's time as a client of Jumbo Johnson Productions is officially over."

"Ooh, I'd never let them do that," he said, his smiling face turning into a mock-serious expression. "But I'm not so sure about that – about Jamie, I mean. I've got a feeling we're gonna see more of her."

Yeah, I had that feeling, too. That we might see more of Jamie in the future. And if we did, well, ... oh boy, oh boy, oh boy!

Epilogue

Six weeks later, Jamie got her first check from Fukknumzie. Nine thousand, one hundred, seventeen dollars and 53 cents. Not a bad start to what looked to be a promising career.

I knew about it because she called me, almost as excited as the first time she got to play with my dick. We talked for about 10 minutes and during that time she must have thanked me a hundred times. The words *oh boy* came up a lot, too.

I'd seen her a couple of times since we'd wrapped up shooting her videos. The Saturday after her final session – the buttfuck video with Megan – she came over to the studio to record some dialogue I could use to replace chatter I'd had to cut out. That usually takes two or three hours but Jamie showed up at around two and didn't leave until after midnight. We, uh, ... got *distracted* and after we finished recording her dialogue, we ended up in the video room, on the bed, and ... well, you know what happened.

She'd also introduced me to her former English teacher, David Glenn, after she'd bumped into him downtown. Davey, as she called him. Dave to everybody else. She brought him to the studio for a prearranged audition on a Sunday afternoon.

Since Dave was a guy, Jamie conducted the audition for me. And she'd been right when she'd told me he'd be a great addition to the *Jumbo Johnson Productions* family. He had the necessary equipment – a dick that was almost as big as mine – and he knew how to use it. He was also a fun guy to be around and, of course, his English was excellent. Not that you needed to be able to speak good English – or be able to speak, at all – to be a porn actor, of course. But still ...

So when she showed up at my apartment, unannounced, about an hour after the phone call that had informed me she was now *rich*, I wasn't all that surprised. But I was torn between feelings of *oh boy!* and *oh no!* It was Saturday, the only day of the week Junior and I got to rest.

And *rest* was seldom on the agenda when Jamie came for a visit. She was so beautiful. And so enthusiastic when it came to sex – *such* a good fuck! I knew I wouldn't be able to resist her.

We ended up in a familiar position – sitting on the couch in my living room, drinking beer and smoking weed. My expectation was that one of Jamie's hands would soon find its way into my pants and that would lead to a trip down the hall to my bedroom and hours and hours of suckyfucky fun. After all, that was the usual outcome when Jamie and I got together.

That's not what happened this time, however. No hand in the pants, no dick squeezing, nothing like that. Instead, she informed me that she wanted to talk business.

Considering the fact that Junior was already doing his stretching exercises, prepping for an afternoon of fun, that news was not exactly what I wanted to hear. "Oh. Okay," I told her, trying not to let my disappointment show on my face.

"Me and Megan have become friends, you know," she began.

"I *do* know. Joey told me. He said the three of you even went out to dinner a couple of weeks ago."

"We did. We went to Tsunami Pizza, that new place down by the beach."

"How was it? Any good?"

"Yeah. Not bad." She paused to take a hit off the joint. "Anyway, so Meg and I have been hanging out, going shopping together and stuff, and we got to talking and decided we wanna do some more videos together."

"Really? With Joey, you mean?"

"No, silly," she said, slapping me on the shoulder. "With *you*. And Joey and Davey, too, of course. We wanna make a series of videos with both of us in them and release one of them each month. But Meg will release the first one and then I'll release the second one and we'll go back and forth, like that. And at the end of each of Meg's videos, there'll be a blurb for the next one, only instead of that next video being on her page, it'll be on mine. And my videos will have blurbs linking back to Meg's page, like that. Our pages will be linked to each other – hopefully, her fans will end up being my fans and vice versa. So, ... whaddaya think?"

"I think that sounds like a great idea."

"Yeah. We thought so, too."

"I'm kinda surprised Joey didn't mention it to me."

"That's probably 'cause Meg and I just came up with this plan yesterday," she said, giggling.

I took a pull off my beer and nodded. "Yup. That's probably why."

"Know what we're thinking about calling our series?"

"Nope. What?"

"Bottom Bangers." A hopeful expression slid across her face. "Whaddaya think? Like it?"

"Yeah, I do." I smiled at her. "Bottom Bangers – very creative. Nice alliteration. Two buttfuck specialists doing their thing."

"Well, that's what guys wanna see now. Girls taking big ones up the butt. You said so, yourself."

"Yup, buttfucking is popular right now. But next year it might be something else, you know."

"Like what?"

I shrugged. Because I'm not psychic – I can't see the future. "Did Meg tell you what she and Joey have been doing? What they think the next big thing might be?"

"I don't think so. What?"

"Piss videos."

"What? What are piss videos?"

"People peeing on each other."

She made a face. "Really?"

"Yup. And at the end, instead of a cum shot, there's usually a pee shot."

"You mean, ...?"

"Yup, right in the mouth."

"Ugh. That's just, ... gross!"

"Sometimes it's the girl peeing in the guy's mouth."

"Still gross."

"You gonna let me pee on you someday, Jaime? Maybe even pee in your mouth?"

She shook her head. "I don't think I'll ever be doing that. I'm pretty sure I don't like piss. I like *cum.*"

"Well, I wouldn't worry about that, sweetie. I see plenty of cum in your future."

We spent the rest of Jamie's visit discussing *logistics*, which basically meant Jamie begging me to sneak her and Megan to the top of my waiting list and me finally agreeing to do it. So instead of having to wait several months for an opening, the *Bottom Bangers* series would be starting production in about three weeks.

And then it was time for Jamie to leave.

"Want me to top you off before I leave?" she said, rubbing her hand across the front of my shorts.

"Top me off?"

"Yeah, you know. Polish your knob for you? Make it all nice and shiny?"

"You mean, ... a blowjob?"

"Some people call it that."

"You in a hurry or something? Someplace you gotta be?"

"Nope. Not really. Why?"

"You wanna fuck, instead?"

"Fuck?" she said, sounding as if she didn't know what the word meant.

"Yeah, that's where I slide my dick in and out of your cunt instead of your mouth."

"Ooh, that sounds like fun. Let's do that." She hopped off the couch, pulled me to my feet, and led me down the hall toward my bedroom. "If you're a good boy, Charlie, maybe I'll even let you fuck that ear of mine you've been eyeing ever since we first met. It's my left one, isn't it? I've seen you staring at it."

"Yeah," I said, laughing as I followed her. "Definitely your left one. It's bigger than your other one – looks more, ... *fuckable!*"

* * *

It was dark by the time Jamie left. Basically, I had to kick her out after fucking her twice. And while I hadn't managed to get my dick into her left ear – or even tried that yet – more Saturday sex was not something I needed. What I really needed was *rest*.

I walked her down to her car – her *new* car, a sleek little Mercedes coupe her dad had bought for her as a high school graduation present, even though she still had a couple of weeks left until she got her diploma. Yup. Being born into a rich family definitely had its perks.

"I'm gonna miss you, Charlie," she said as she buckled herself in and started the car.

"See you in three weeks," I told her, kissing her goodbye.

"Who knows? Maybe even sooner." She laughed and drove away.

I watched as the car taillights disappeared down the road, then went back upstairs. Fucking Jamie was – and probably always would be – lots of fun. But at the time, there was something that appealed to me even more than the idea of having her drain my dick of cum. And that something was called, ... sleep.

the end – fini – owari

Oh boy, oh boy, oh boy! Some girls are sure a lot of fun. Unfortunately, Jamie's story is over. But if you liked this book, I have three other series available at your favorite online bookseller that may interest you. They include:

<u>The Waikiki Hummer Adventures</u> – Meet Terry Jean Rollins, a young Honolulu girl whose 'hobby' involves the dicks of middle-aged, dorky male visitors to Waikiki ... and humming.

<u>The Mike and Melanie Escapades</u> – Adventures of a young, swinging couple (and their sex-obsessed neighbor, Nikki, who joins the series in Book 2, appropriately titled, <u>New Neighbor Nikki</u>).

<u>Pleasantly Plump</u> – A nasty romance series, featuring girls who are just a teeny-tiny bit on the plump side and are looking to lose 5-10 pounds.

All of the books in these series are standalone stories with no cliffhangers and can be read in any order. However, as is typical with series fiction, reading them in order is recommended for maximum enjoyment.

Well, that's it. I hope you enjoyed the book. Please leave a review if you have time – I'd <u>really</u> appreciate that. See ya soon, I hope!
See ya soon! Hugs and kisses. Shannon

Milton Keynes UK
Ingram Content Group UK Ltd.
UKHW020615071223
433828UK00014B/642